TRANSPLANT

By D.J. Hamlin

Northern Star Publishing, Minneapolis, Minnesota 2020

Northern Star Publishing, 2020
KDP Publishing, 2020

Series: Author D.J. Hamlin, Transplant, Fiction, 1st Edition.

Paperback ISBN   978-1-7332796-4-2

eBook ISBN 13: 978-1-7332796-5-9

TRANSPLANT

Chapter One

The call came in a minute after one thirty in the morning on a cold, dark Minnesota evening. The shrill noise startled Seth Emerson from a deep slumber, the kind that overtakes a person on a blustery, frozen January night. The alarm continued to ring until he hit the switch to acknowledge the call; he let out a choice cuss word as he rolled up to his feet and began moving swiftly across the cold, tile floor and out into the corridor.

"Emma! Em! We gotta move, we got a live one on the line!"

He used a fishing reference, the kind he liked best from his many summers in a boat on a beautiful, blue Minnesota lake. He stumbled as he pulled on his pants, trying to make himself presentable to his boss, the lady surgeon in the other room.

"Em! Em! Get up…we gotta fly!"

He began knocking on the door and she responded groggily but with volume. "I'm up…we can roll in two minutes!" Within three minutes they were inside their vehicle and out of the open double garage door.

Seth drove and Emma made radio contact with the law officers assigned to the call.

"A wreck off of County 34, north of town...go out Richwood road, it'll be quickest."

She was on her computer, calculating the drive time to the scene and possible harvest situation. The large vehicle looked like a motor home that a tourist would use to go camping in during the sultry summer months, but this was an all-together different set up. This was a harvest station on wheels that revolutionized the medical profession.

The young doctor powered the huge, white operating room on wheels at a pace that would seem dangerous to most people. His veteran boss and fellow surgeon, Emma Harris, barely looked up from her computer to show concern. The duo had made this type of run many times over the last year and had driven as fast in conditions that were much worse. She had all the faith in the world concerning her fellow surgeon's abilities to drive the beast of a vehicle. They had danced this dance many times before and were among the top doctors in their new field.

The specialists drove deep into the countryside in the darkness. The rural roads were temporarily illuminated by glowing lights from farm yards along the way. As they moved through a small blink-and-you-will-miss-it town, they took a right and headed further out. After a quarter mile they saw an array of flashing lights and emergency vehicles and Emma, who had been on the radio, signed off.

"Troy Haley says to pull up past the curve, there is a space on the right that he has cleared for us, right in front of the ambulance. Watch it past the fire rig, there's a lot of people mulling around. Apparently this is a big deal."

The driver slowed and maneuvered around the crowd of emergency workers that spanned part of the way into the road.

"Any idea what our chances are of a harvest?" he asked as his blood got pumping and his curiosity started peaking.

"Troy thinks that its good, the victim passed within the last five minutes and they did their best to stabilize the body. He's pretty good at what he does."

The surgery van pulled into the prescribed spot at the edge of the snowy road and Seth opened up the back. Emma moved quickly to the scene and asked officer Haley for an update.

"Just got him out...victim is a male, approximately fifty-five, Caucasian. Nice vehicle... a Mercedes, newer model. He must've lost it on the curve. Weird though, no ice. We have no toxicology on him yet...maybe drunk."

Emma frowned a little bit at the last statement.

"Damn, I hope not, that would screw everything up."

She moved to the ambulance where the freshly deceased was laid on a stretcher in the back.

7

"Let's transfer now, let's move him out." The surgeon directed to the paramedics.

"Yes, doctor." They echoed in reverence to her stature and reputation.

It took twenty seconds to move the victim from one vehicle to the other and Seth quickly shut the door behind them. The engine on the portable surgery center started to idle at a higher rate of RPM's as they switched on power to all of the machines needed in the operation. A blood circulator was quickly hooked into the victim to keep the brain alive.

"We have to move quick, there's no telling how long we have."

Seth nodded at the command from his boss and replied "They said five to ten minutes… should be a viable window for us yet. God I love this stuff."

The small hand-held power saw flipped into motion and the Seth began his part of the process. The surgeon took precaution to cut up under the hairline; someone might want an open casket funeral and he didn't want to make it look like the victim had been scalped. He cut quickly, moving carefully through the skull and into the cranial cavity. The top of the man's head came off after about forty-five seconds.

Emma reached over to the jugular vein on the left side of the victim and flipped off the switch that moved blood to the head and brain area of the victim.

"We're off, you have two minutes starting now."

With the small device turned off, the blood began to drain very quickly from the head into the torso.

"Perfect. Let's get it out carefully. Get the stabilizer ready...cool it down slowly, set it at four."

The lead doctor was now on the clock as her assistant readied the machine that would keep the organ viable.

"Hey, it looks good. Nice job with the cut."

She needed to talk as she worked, it actually helped her to concentrate and stay steady. There were some surgeries where she spent the better part of five minutes talking about professional football or the latest cooking show she had seen. On this night she was a little tired and so talking would turn out to be more exhausting. The dialogue died down quickly.

With skillful, intricate scalpel work the main connection to the spinal cord was carefully severed and the final blood vessels were cut. Using tender care, Doctor Harris reached in and lifted the brain out of the dead man's skull. She slowly turned and placed it in the stabilizer as Seth added the mineral fluid that would keep the organ in pristine condition.

"That, my friend, never ceases to amaze me." She said with pride and wonder, smiling at her accomplishment.

Chapter Two

Ten Years Earlier

He woke up when he heard the crunching of gravel under the tires as the truck came to a reckless halt. A beer bottle skittered across the gravel, not breaking but instead bouncing with an obnoxious clanking. A light or two flipped on in a dirty, worn out neighborhood in the middle of nowhere. The man of the house was coming home and, as was custom, was drunk again.

The boy sat up as a shudder ran through his body, not knowing what to expect and a sense of sudden fear gripped at his young mind. He didn't like the man; the man scared him every day. He would sit, sometimes for the better part of an hour, wondering why his mom would let the man stay in their home.

The wooden door slammed hard, shattering the silence of the night inside the small townhome. Erratic footsteps thundered down the dark, narrow hallway past his room; he was safe for a moment. The heavy door to the bedroom next to his thundered open and he could hear the man yelling loudly, then his mom began to scream.

The little boy moved cautiously toward his bedroom door and opened it slowly. The hall was empty but the door next to his was wide open and he could hear crashing and screaming coming from within. He snuck along the worn wall and peeked his head into the chaos, recoiling with horror while seeing the man slamming his fist into his mom.

Fury overtook the youngster's mind and he rushed into the room to save the only person in the world who cared for him. The drunk was busy beating up his girlfriend for no apparent reason other than the fact that he could and did not see the boy approaching. The kid was tough for a five-year-old. He had been bullied most of his life in the tenement of trashed townhomes.

Moving as fast as his short legs would allow him, he latched onto the man's right leg with both hands and sunk his teeth into the blue jean covered limb. The boy bit with all of his might and the drunk screamed with pain. The big man spun sideways and the child held on, his teeth digging into fabric and flesh.

The young child was forced to give up his grip when the man grabbed him by the hair and lifted him into the air. The tiny body flew across the room and made a dent in the sheetrock wall before bouncing face down on the floor. The monster attacked quickly despite being impaired; he had fought while inebriated before. The woman was weeping and blood ran down from her scalp; he had landed some powerful punches before the little kid showed up.

The drunken bully covered the distance between himself and the boy in three long strides. On the third kick to the head, the boy blacked out. His mother was screaming even louder as she tried to tackle the aggressor and he stopped beating the senseless child.

****

A week had passed and the young victim lay unconscious in his sterile, dim hospital room. His mother left his side only to get water, food, or take a bathroom break. The nurses felt a special sympathy for her that could only be fathomed in a small-town regional hospital. Country folk could always count on each other when times were tough and this was one of the toughest times that a mother could go through.

The nurses whispered around their work station in the center of the ICU as they felt pity for the beaten woman and her dying son. Sympathetic wagers were made on how long the young boy would survive and he surprised all of them; not a single caregiver gave him a week of life after seeing him wheeled in from surgery with his skull partially destroyed. He was a fighter, a tough little kid, and the few people who really knew him would never bet against him.

Days turned to weeks and, one sunny morning when the birds were singing their spring praises, the young boy woke up. His eyes opened very slowly as they adjusted to the painful light; his head pounded with pain and he turned to recognize his mom in the bright surroundings.

"Momma."

It took all of his energy to whisper toward the woman sitting half asleep in the chair by his bedside.

"Oh my God! Travis! Oh my baby!"

The nurse on duty heard the screaming and approached the room in a sprint. There was no flashing trauma light, what could be the problem?

She slowed as she crossed the threshold to the room and smiled as tears began to fill her eyes and roll down her cheeks. He was awake, the little boy had made it. The mother held her small son in her arms and wept tears of joy as well; this was surely a miracle. The boy tried to hug his mother back but there was no coordination or strength in his arms. He just lay against her and felt great relief flood his brain. He was alive!

Chapter Three

Up to Present Day

Kindergarten arrived at the beginning of September and Travis made his way to school with his mother holding his hand. It was only three blocks from the school; they had moved to a much better location after leaving the dingy townhome complex on the other side of town.

The young boy had a perpetual smile on his face, in fact it never left. He never seemed to get mad about anything and was always in a world all his own. As they reached the classroom door in the old brick structure, his mother hesitated as she worried about his well-being.

There was nothing to worry about. Travis was clueless to the world around him. He could hear what others were saying and could try to participate in conversation, but sometimes he would become confused and there were some instances where the words that came out of his mouth didn't match the words that his brain was trying to say. This could produce a chuckle from some of the kids in his new neighborhood and he was all right with this, it helped him feel accepted by his friends.

The kindergarten year flew by and Travis was a bit of a celebrity within the grade school. Most of the kids seemed to take a liking to him and those that didn't were quickly put in their place. Bullies would try to make fun of him but Travis was fortunate to have the biggest kid in the kindergarten class, a smart boy named Ray, as his best friend. Ray came from a family of six boys that ranged from him as the youngest to his oldest brother Scott, a junior in high school. Nobody would be messing with Travis without feeling the pain of retribution from the boys.

Everybody moved on to first grade except Travis. Teachers met with his mother and gently explained what she already knew, that her son was way behind in aptitude from his peers. She took the time to explain it to him and he grasped very little of what she meant; it became somewhat of an award to him to have a do-over in Ms. Smith's kindergarten class. As she maneuvered her way through this difficult situation, fraught with guilt, she also stayed diligent in her appointments with the neurological doctors who continued to work for the benefit of her son.

Travis slowly made his way through elementary school with the help and dedication of the special education teachers who devoted all the time they possibly could to his learning and improvement of cognitive skills. The young man remained well-liked as he entered his awkward junior high school years and by ninth grade was something of a celebrity among his peers. His junior year found him at the area high school and his celebrity status was diminished; it was a much bigger building with more students and he was suddenly lost in the crowd.

A simple fact remained however, he was still functioning at a level where he would never be able to live on his own or take care of himself. He would always need special help.

****

The meeting started the way a typical education meeting starts, with everyone sitting around a table introducing themselves. The group leader slowly read aloud as they worked their way through the Individualized Education report that had been prepared and revised over the many years of Travis' schooling.

The facts within the documents never really seemed to change much because Travis really never seemed to change. Life was more difficult now with all the trials and tribulations of young adulthood upon the disabled young man. The meeting came to a screeching halt when the school psychologist turned the subject to science.

"Mrs. Adamson, has anyone talked to you about reconstructive brain surgery?"

Travis' mom froze with a confused look on her face.

"Reconstructive what?" she replied, almost in jest yet curious at the professional's comment.

"Reconstructive surgery to restore the cognitive processes of the brain. It can range from repairable surgery with the existing organ to a full or partial transplant of the brain. You've never heard of it?"

Everyone around the table sat in silence, some bound with curiosity, others wondering if this was some kind of cruel joke.

"I'm sorry...I have no idea of what you are talking about." The mother responded with utter confusion, feeling stupid. The professional continued.

"In today's medical community, we are harvesting brain matter and full organs from the diseased for transplant into qualifying candidates who need or desire a new beginning. Many of the candidates are similar to your son. They have experienced severe trauma and have no options left to help them out. This process, which is actually quite complex, is a new beginning for many people like Travis."

She looked across the table at the balding psychologist and, with an indignant glare, responded to the counselor.

"You're kidding, right? Are you out of your cotton-picking mind? A freaking brain transplant? That's the craziest thing I have ever heard!"

The puzzled and frustrated mother scanned the room, checking the reactions of all of the people in the meeting. Everyone averted their eyes or kept their heads down. Nobody dared to weigh in on this topic, it was too new and controversial to many people in this day and age.

"I have a book in my office that talks about this new medical breakthrough...I will let you borrow it if you'd like. I know people in the cities... at the University. They specialize in this procedure. I'm sorry if I have offended or confused you...I just think this could really help Travis."

Nobody else at the table said a word; the silence was deafening.

"Just take the book home and give it a quick read. It might be just the thing you are looking for."

The skeptical mother chuckled lightly and said in a non-believing whisper, "We'll see."

She spent every night for over a week reading about the new medical breakthroughs and every night she went to sleep harboring a little more hope for her boy. The school psychologist was onto something and the more she read, the more she believed. Communication was made with the University of Minnesota Hospital and an appointment was scheduled in Minneapolis over Travis' Christmas break.

Sylvia Adamson met with more doctors than she could keep track of during her visit to the cities. The medical campus was very user friendly and people from their hometown of Waterloo, Iowa donated enough money to pay for a week's worth of hotel rooms.

The information was overwhelming at times, so much of it was laced with medical jargon and diagrams that it was hard to follow, but one thing was certain. This new medical process could give her son the kind of life that she had robbed him of when she took up with the drunk boyfriend so many years earlier.

"I owe it to him to give him a chance at a real life. I made one mistake that ruined his life, I have a chance to make it right."

The many papers needed to give medical consent for the procedure were signed and testing began on the fourth day that they were in town. The doctors seemed to know their profession well, everything was done in a quick but thorough manner and the Adamsons returned to Waterloo with a new set of dates on their calendar. Travis would be revisiting the University of Minnesota hospital during the first week of February. If things went well, he would be returning to Iowa a new man; if things went wrong he would be returning home in a casket.

Chapter Four

The doctors at the university examined the new brain very carefully as they knew exactly what they were looking for. Any abnormalities, any fissures showing damage, any dead spots, and the surgery would be called off. Dr. Harris had made her way down to the cities with her specimen and was considered a pioneer in this type of research.

Years before she had completed her undergraduate work at the U along with grad work in Minneapolis, then she moved on to Johns Hopkins University in Baltimore for her formal medical training. A two-year stint at Georgetown University for extended medicine and surgery placed her in the company of an elite few in the medical world.

She had then helped to create the process that had been used in harvesting the brain in Northern Minnesota. She had also pioneered the process of installing the organ in a living human being. Everyone who was someone in the neurosurgery world considered her to be one of the top doctors in the country…a woman with few peers.

"Dr. Stuart, take a look at this." She remarked casually to a fellow surgeon who would complete most of the transplant process.

"There are hardly any damage marks, no calcification, no clots…this might be the most perfect brain we have worked with yet. I would guess the guy has never smoked a day in his life…probably drank little alcohol as well. This thing is BEAUTIFUL."

She made the last exclamation with a touch of wonderment because in her world, it was truly a thing a beauty.

"Damn, you're right, it is indeed a beautiful organ. Have you had a chance to meet the young man we will be working with tomorrow morning?"

She moved her head back and forth indicating the negative.

"No, I will be going upstairs later today to say hello. From what I understand he is quite a nice kid."

Stuart nodded with a smile.

"You are going to like him, his name is Travis and he has a great sense of humor… if you can understand what he is saying. If we do this right we will be giving him a new lease on life."

Dr. Emma Harris smiled warmly to herself. "We had better do this right then."

The good doctor finished up her work with the transplant organ and stowed it away carefully. If all went as planned the brain would be inside Travis Adamson's head within thirty-six hours.

She stopped at her station and retrieved her lunch from a small, white fridge off the main area. A five-minute walk found her in the midst of the hospital cafeteria, bustling with activity. Emma usually liked to eat alone, but she learned that a surgery like the one she was about to undertake meant many hours of isolation from the general public. As a result, on this day she preferred to dine with people.

The wise doctor always made it a habit to pass on the cafeteria food as it usually disagreed with her. Nobody wanted to work with a surgeon who had a bad case of gas or worse yet, diarrhea.

Emma recognized no one and ended up eating at a table all alone. She opened up her container of lettuce and chicken spread and ate it faster than she should have; she felt uneasy eating at a table alone. She remembered how sorry she felt for the poor, miserable, lonely eaters in her high school cafeteria many years earlier. Now she wondered how many people felt that way about her.

Dr. Harris was supposed to make her way upstairs to meet her patient, Travis Adamson. She knew she would not keep the appointment, that was why she made sure that Dr. Stuart had visited.

The surgeon wanted no part of meeting with her patient because meeting Travis would build up a relationship... a knowledge of who she was working on, and she didn't want that. She did not want the guilt to hang over her if things went poorly. At this point in the process he was just a body that needed repair. She would take the time to get to know him after the surgery, a victory celebration of sorts.

Emma made sure to keep her one o'clock meeting with the surgery team up in the main conference room off of the operating room. They would walk through the procedure step by step and then practice out in the room. Game day would be the next morning at seven, they would have a small break at noon, and then they would continue until finished, probably somewhere around nine or ten at night. One never knew the timeline for sure, one complication could set them back an hour or more, no complications and they might be done early. Dr. Emma Harris lived for game day.

The meeting in the conference room started right on time. It went surprisingly quick, followed by a standard walk through of the surgery. Harris then returned to the conference room with Dr. Stuart to walk over the fine details and any potential problems that they would have to address. They took seats across the mahogany table from each other and she began to outline the details.

"As we saw earlier, there shouldn't be any problems with the organ. Everything looks exceptional and there are great contact points for the tissue splices and relay. I'm going to use the cross-relay process to place the device, I think that it will function better for a longer period of time and there seems to be an abundance of tissue to secure to. Are you familiar with the Kruitsman process for tissue merge?"

She looked her colleague in the eyes, hoping he had studied up.

He had a blank look on his face, he was caught without doing his homework. She continued.

"Dr. David Kruitsman. Georgetown Med. He took four years to perfect the process, it wasn't easy."

She looked at him the whole time with hope that something would register. Stuart smiled back at her with an inquiring look.

"Kruitsman? You sound like you know him...did you study his techniques at G.U.?"

Emma smiled back at the seemingly confused doctor for a moment, not knowing what to say.

"Um, Stu...I helped develop the process in my internship with him. I spent the last year of the process working on it WITH HIM!"

The doctor blushed as he was caught not knowing about the procedure or his colleague.

"You're shitting me, right?" he replied with a smile, stunned at what he had just learned.

"I shit you not, Stu. I was working with him and Jane on it." Stu smiled wider.

"Jane? As in Jane Culligan? THEE Jane Culligan?"

The unprepared doctor was laughing out loud now, partly from embarrassment and partly from amazement.

"Stu?" she continued, now having fun with him, "Jane Culligan was my supervising surgeon for two years."

He continued to chuckle while shaking his head. "Is she as big of a bitch as everyone says?"

Emma was laughing lightly now, wondering just how to tactfully answer the obvious.

"I wouldn't say a bitch, at least not every day. She was tough to please and she really pushed those who could tolerate working with her. I will say this, though. I learned more from her in two years than from anyone else in my life. It was worth the headaches and, believe me, there were a lot of them!"

Dr. Stuart was eating up this information, feeling like he was learning classified information.

"Damn, I'm working with a celebrity!"

Dr. Emma just smiled. Normally she would chastise him for using such off-color language. Not this time though, sometimes it was fun to be someone famous and to name drop!

They broke up the meeting at three-thirty, confident that they had tomorrow perfected down to the minute. The good doctor held true to her belief that meeting the patient was in poor taste for her superstition and she decided to head to her hotel suite for plenty of rest. Tomorrow would be a big day.

****

The sun came up at about the time the doctors and their team went into surgery. There was an excitement in the air that could only be rivaled by a sports team entering the stadium for a championship contest. Everyone was ready and the positive attitudes flowed through the prep room and the surgical center itself.

The gallery above was full with fellow surgeons and medical students who all realized that this was not a typical run of the mill event. This operation would be something special. The news media had found out about this extraordinary happening but the hospital security kept them well away. Dr. Emma Harris and her team did not need any distractions at a moment like this. They had work to do.

Travis Adamson was wheeled on a gurney into the operating room, already stone cold out with sedation. He would not have any memory or awareness of what would take place, to him it was just another day.

As hard as his mother worked to try and explain what would happen, he understood none of it. He just spent his days in a peaceful melancholy, unaware of anything around him except smiling people who were always nice to him. He had his friends who understood his predicament and that was all he needed. If the young man survived the ordeal his life would never be the same.

It took the first hour just to hook Travis up to all the machines that would keep him alive throughout the process. From respiration to cardio and blood flow, he himself would be a machine for a major part of the process. It didn't matter though, what mattered was that he would come out of the operation alive and hopefully, in good health.

There were many things that could possibly go wrong but most of the hurdles had been jumped in the past; the doctors handling this operation were ready for most anything that might happen, good or bad.

Dr. Stuart handled the first part of the procedure as he was in charge of opening Travis up and assessing the current state of the brain. This part of the morning proved to be more difficult than they anticipated because of all the trauma that Travis' brain had endured. The damage had been extensive, particularly to the skull structure itself and certain regions on one side of his brain.

Dr. Harris spent a considerable amount of the morning using a microscope and checking most of the critical areas of the organ that she would be working with. After two hours of intense scrutiny she concluded that there was enough matter to splice to and use stem cells on.

Most of Travis' brain would be removed and studied for further research projects at the University. About one third of his working brain, including some memory centers would be harvested and attached onto the new organ after implant in his skull. He would be two-thirds new and one-third old Travis. This would hopefully ensure that he would keep some memory from his past life along with clearing most of his disabilities.

An electronic device would aid in the transfer of information and the working of the two organs together; it was this device that Emma had worked on with her famous doctors back at Georgetown and Johns Hopkins.

When the proper time arrived, Dr. Stuart removed Travis' brain, severing the right connections and removing it for further dissection. Placing it in a shallow basin with the proper chemical solution, he began to carefully prepare the existing third of the brain that would be spliced with the new organ.

Dr. Harris took over, setting the new organ in Travis' cranium and making the connections that would get blood back to the transplant. It seemed like an hour to those watching in the gallery but, in reality, the procedure took about half that time.

The initial connections were in place and Emma checked the blood flow and pulse. Everything worked the way it was supposed to and she smiled while informing the team and the gallery that the new organ was in place and viable. Light cheers went up from the gallery but she could not hear them as the glass windows kept her environment isolated from the viewers. Stu, working at the table next to her offered a quiet, but heartfelt congratulations.

The afternoon turned to early evening as the process carried on uneventfully. Harris was almost surprised that there were no problems, she had anticipated at least something difficult. The young age of the patient worked to their favor and he seemed to be one strong kid.

The splice, cells, and device were in and Travis' skull was closed after six that evening. Now the waiting would begin and for Emma this was always the toughest part; one never knew what would work and what would not until weeks later when everything was taking hold and not being rejected.

"This went really well, I think it could be our best work yet. Time to pray." she muttered to herself as she left the sanitary area and headed to locker room for a shower.

Chapter Five

"Will he ever remember me?" Sylvia Adamson asked with trepidation, hoping for an affirmative answer.

"It's difficult to say. We have had patients regain memory two or three years after the surgery. We can't be sure that what we transplanted took hold, or for that matter, if what was in there before has survived. We can only guess."

Dr. Harris was trying to be as positive as possible but she came off as evasive to the mother and son.

"He remembers his friends at school. Now he can talk to them and relate to them...he's just like them. I do not understand why he can't remember me?"

An uncomfortable silence fell over the room as everyone looked toward Travis. The young man had emerged from an induced coma a month before, totally confused at his surroundings and the people he came in contact with. He hadn't returned to school or home yet, instead his closest friends had made the trip up from Waterloo to say hello and see how he was doing. He remembered Ray the minute he walked into the room and his friend was so flattered he started tearing up.

"From past experience, we have found that everything takes time. Memories from his own life will come back in spurts along with memories stored by the person before him. He will go through a period of time, sooner or later, where he will take on the persona and memories of the person who donated the organ. How he comes out of this, we don't know. But we were all aware of the risks going in, right Mrs. Adamson?"

The mother shook her head gently as she looked over her son sitting upright next to her. "I just want a normal life for him."

****

Travis didn't say much, but one thing was certain, he was gaining more control of his speech every day. He began to notice subtle things around him and he took note of the fact that his mouth said exactly what his brain wanted it to. He found this exciting and fun and would turn on the radio in his room and sing to whatever came on. The teen used to know the words to the pop songs of the day but could not be able to get them out of his mouth; now they were coming out like a rock star and he was enjoying every verse.

Everything changed one morning, just over two months after the surgery, when sitting up in his hospital bed he blurted out the St. John's University fight song in perfect pitch. "Fight you Johnnies, Fight you Johnnies, Stand and Fight like men for Old St. John's....". He sang the whole song for two hours until the nurses finally had heard enough and told him to stop. They turned on his radio to a heavy metal station, hoping it would distract him. Their tactic didn't work for very long, within fifteen minutes he was back to the fight song.

A couple of days later the morning nurse said hello to him and he didn't recognize his name. "Who's Travis?" he asked with a straight face. The nurse stopped in her tracks and pointed to him with a confused look on her face.

"I'm Bruce. I don't know a Travis. Did he used to be in this room?"

The rookie caretaker ran to the nurse's station and dialed up Dr. Stuart. He arrived within the hour and began asking questions of his patient.

"Good morning young man, how are you today?" he began. The patient smiled and responded kindly.

"You flatter me doctor, really…young man? I'm older than you realize." He chuckled and the doctor showed puzzlement.

"What's your name, sir?" Stuart asked with a straight face.

"Isn't it there on the chart? On the door to my room? Bruce Nickel, like the money!"

Stu was stunned, he had heard of this happening but it was his first time encountering it in person.

"Well, Mr. Nickel, how are we treating you here?"

Mr. Nickel gave him a thumbs up and went back to singing the Johnnie fight song. The doctor ducked out of the room and dialed his colleague as confusion dominated his mind.

"Emma. Stu here in Minneapolis...how are you doing?"

She was surprised to hear from her friend in the cities; they had spoken the day before and she couldn't imagine anything new to talk about.

"Are you sitting down?" he asked with a hint of humor in his voice.

"What did YOU do?" she asked, humor in her tone as well.

"It's about our friend Travis Adamson, or should I say Bruce Nickel." Emma was confused for a second and then her mind kicked in.

"Bruce Nickel, huh? That's the name of the brain we transplanted...I harvested it myself from a crash scene up in Becker county last January." There was a short silence on the other end of the line and then Stu spoke up.

"Is this kind of thing common?" he asked with curiosity. Harris knew the answer, she had seen this before, in fact it was to be expected.

"Stu, this is totally normal. Every transplant we have done goes through this faze...sometimes is lasts a long time, sometimes is wears off quickly. There is no way of knowing how long the brain will hold on to its original identity…we suspect that the person overrides the old personality with their new one as it develops. Kind of crazy, right?"

They continued their conversation for a few minutes and then they went back to the rigors of their day. Dr. Emma kept thinking about the young man sitting in a hospital room in the Twin Cities and she made a note to try and schedule a visit sometime near the end of the month. She didn't see any reason to worry about the present situation, as she reiterated to herself that this was all part of the game.

"The kid made it. He's alive. We win!"

Chapter Six

"Ed, we have a problem. The insurance company doesn't want to pay out on the claim. They said something about finishing an investigation. I want my money NOW!"

The blonde trophy wife screamed the last word into her phone for added emphasis. She was the high maintenance woman that every man wanted but few men could afford.

"Don't worry babe. This stuff takes time. Just lay low and let the process happen...we don't need anybody poking around."

She threw a small temper tantrum as she hung up her phone and gazed at the sandy beach and sparkling, clear water.

Fast Eddie Payne was bothered by the fact that she wouldn't shut up. He didn't want to have to shut her up, she was so damn hot and so good for him. He would miss her if he had to kill her, but sometimes you had to wipe out a possible threat. He leaned back in his office chair and surveyed the downtown scene in the big city.

"Damn, I'd rather be there with her...the things we could be doing...hmmm."

He had a black book full of women's phone numbers and he could be with any of them within an hour's time, provided their husbands or boyfriends weren't home.

"All in a day's work…the perils of being Fast Eddie."

He could stick around the office and try to pick up one of the young secretaries or he could try and get some work done. Work was not an option because work was not fun. He could run downstairs and across the street to the Irish bar on the corner and try his luck there.

"Irish, luck, huh, huh, huh…" he laughed to himself, it was almost a guaranteed hit if he worked over there. He thought to himself that maybe he should stay faithful to Faith, his blonde bombshell girlfriend vacationing at the Florida villa. He let out a laugh loud enough to attract the attention of the people outside of his office door, and then he headed across the street.

****

Travis was sitting up in bed, watching Wheel of Fortune because it was his favorite show. He remembered that. He used to like to sit and watch the wheel spin and look at the pretty girl who pointed at letters, now he was enjoying solving the puzzles. He still thought he was Bruce and became confused every time someone called him Travis.

In the middle of the puzzle he had a flashback. His mind drifted away and he felt like he was suddenly in an old movie. He was driving his car on a dark road, and he stopped for gasoline at a small general store. He could picture the aged white store with its wooden porch so clearly. It was night and very cold; small snowflakes were gently falling from the sky.

He put the gas nozzle back on the pump and tucked his card back in his wallet. He looked into the dark store from the pumps and shuddered, a cold cup of coffee would have been good if the establishment had been open. The car was nice, it had a leather interior and was warm.

He took a quick right out of the station lot and hooked another quick right onto a road that led to nowhere in particular. He passed a dark, strange looking church and suddenly the car took off on him. It accelerated and he couldn't get it to stop; pushing on the brakes did nothing. The steering wheel spun and the last thing he saw as he approached the curve was a big oak coming straight at him.

Travis let out a scream, not realizing that he was in another world. It was like a strange dream and the nurses came running to check on the chaos. He was shaking and crying as they entered the room, and then, like flipping a light switch on, his mind returned to the room and the game show. The young man was embarrassed when he saw the nurses approaching to comfort him.

"I'm alright, I'm alright." he repeated over and over while the nurses called for a doctor. A young intern answered the call to the room and brushed it off as a bad dream within thirty seconds of his arrival. He had better things to do than hang out with a teenager having a nightmare.

Travis went to bed that evening and had difficulty falling asleep. He kept replaying the sequence of scenes that ran through his mind earlier, not having a clue of what any of it meant. He just knew that when the sequence was finished he was physically sick and felt the urge to vomit all over the room. Sleep finally took over his brain and he drifted into a new movie.

He was driving in the summer time and he saw the small, white store again, this time with people coming in and out. A middle-aged gentleman with dark, thinning hair and round rimmed glasses was waiving at him from the wooden porch and he felt like he knew him. A large, burly man with a graying goatee and a dark Australian hat was calling out to him and he waived in that man's direction as well.

He jumped back into the dark sedan with the leather seats and the air conditioning felt good. He roared around the corner and up the road he recognized from earlier, but now it was light and he saw the church at the top of the hill.

The luxury automobile turned onto a gravel road and followed it through a curve to a large, blue house. Pulling into the driveway, he felt the sensation of being happy to be home. *Bruce felt alive.*

As he entered the dwelling, a beautiful blonde woman approached him in a bikini that was easily two sizes too small and she rushed to him and planted a kiss on his cheek. He wanted more, a lot more. As she pivoted back to her chair on the sunny deck, he got a great look at her tremendous figure and he felt like he owned the world.

Travis awoke in a sweat and it took a moment for him to realize that it was all a dream. It seemed so real, like it happened right there and now. But that was impossible for the room was dark and quiet. The light from the bathroom in the corner was the only illumination besides the dim light entering from outside.

He took a moment to swing his legs over the side of the bed and, with some effort, he walked to the window and looked out. Travis recognized very few of the local landmarks but he enjoyed the nighttime view and the traffic flowing below. He lost track of time and before he knew it the sun was coming up over the horizon.

Hours later Travis was awakened by a soft touch on his left forearm. He was disoriented for a moment and glanced over to the clock on the stand to his right.

"Twelve-thirty-seven. It's light out. Man, I slept a long time."

"Hello Travis, how is my favorite patient?" Dr. Harris spoke softly in a friendly tone, not wanting to startle him.

"I'm ok, Doc. Why does everyone call me Travis?"

She smiled and sat down on the edge of the bed, not quite the proper etiquette for a surgeon of her regard.

"We talked about this, remember? Your new brain thinks it's someone else, but you are really Travis Adamson from Waterloo, Iowa. Remember now?"

He looked at her with a funny expression.

"I think I like being Bruce Nickel better. I had another dream last night, after the scary one. I really liked the second dream better."

He proceeded to tell her about the summer dream with the beautiful woman at the blue house and she got a bit of a chuckle out of it. *"Teenage boys, always dreaming about girls."*

After a standard examination that took a quarter of an hour, Dr. Harris left the room and checked Travis' vitals on the charts at the nurse's station. Everything seemed normal and the young patient's progress looked great. Another week and he would be free to return to the cornfields of Iowa. Things could not have been better.

As she drove out of the parking lot and headed back to the freeway and her drive to the northland, she began to think about the dream that Travis had described back in his room.

"It's common for the patient to experience flashbacks from the former life of the brain. Is he dreaming, or is this a series of recollections of things that actually happened? What was the scary dream about? Damn it, I should have asked him to explain it."

The doctor's curiosity was killing her and she took the closest exit and returned to the hospital. As she walked into the room, she walked into Travis having another dream.

She watched the young man, writhing in his bed, seeming to be in a struggle or in pain and she didn't bother to interrupt the sequence. He woke suddenly, startled by the surroundings and her presence in the room.

"Travis, honey, what were you dreaming about?" she asked in a soft voice.

"Don't call me TRAVIS! I am BRUCE!" he yelled at the top of his voice. A nurse ran in to investigate and backed off when she saw Dr. Harris sitting in a chair next to the bed.

"Is everything ok?" she asked with concern.

"Everything is fine. Bruce is just waking up."

The nurse looked at the patient with confusion and then decided not to pursue it. If the doctor was there it was good enough for her.

"So, Bruce...what were you dreaming about?" The teenager sat up in bed and struggled to get a hold of his thoughts.

"I think it was the same thing as last night...a car crash."

Dr. Harris' interest was piqued, she hadn't heard this dream. The young man took two minutes to describe it in the best detail that he could and when he finished she sat there staring at him, her face ashen. He had just described the crash scene where she had harvested his transplant brain.

Chapter Seven

"Ms. Adamson, this is Doctor Harris at University Children's unit."

The doctor was interrupted by a concerned mother who had endured her limits regarding her son's health situation.

"Is everything OK?" she blurted in a heightened state, worried about bad news.

"Yes Sylvia, everything is great. Travis is making progress everyday...we are amazed at how well he is doing." The anxious mother let down her guard and began to breathe again.

"The reason I am calling is that I would like to transfer him north for further rehabilitation, specifically in detailed aspects of rehab. I think this will get him back home and in the classroom even quicker."

Sylvia Adamson was willing to do anything to speed her son's recovery.

"Where would you be taking him?"

The doctor saw this response as positive and launched into her plan.

"We would be transferring to a hospital in Twin Lakes…they have a speech pathologist that is an old friend of mine. She's very good, among the best at what she does and I think she can work on ways to stimulate his brain through speech to hasten the splice between his old brain and the new transplant."

It didn't take long for the mother to give consent and within fifteen minutes Doctor Harris was arranging transport of her patient to Northern Minnesota.

Despite a distance of two hundred miles, the ambulance transport was easy to arrange; Emma had all the right connections in the medical world. By late afternoon Travis was on his way to the north.

The move was not as complicated as one would think because most of the tubes and machines had been taken weeks ago. Pain meds and anti-rejection drugs were in pill form and so he was very mobile; he enjoyed the ride in the back of the vehicle while trying to figure out a small, handheld video game.

"What the heck do kids see in this stuff?" he pondered to himself as he became electronically addicted.

The hospital admittance crew got Travis checked into the room after normal visiting hours and they spared no luxury. He had a large room with a big screen television all to himself and the bed seemed more comfortable than back in Minneapolis. He would learn the next day from many visitors and curious onlookers that he was something of a celebrity due to being one of a few people to recover from this procedure so quickly. Dr. Harris checked in with the new patient over the lunch hour the next day as she had a late night from more harvesting in Fargo, North Dakota.

With two days of therapy complete, none of which seemed very fun to the new patient, the doctor made plans to take Travis for a little drive. Proper clearance was submitted and approved and parental support was gained; now Dr. Emma would commence with her experiment. Worst case scenario could mean a major setback and trauma, middle of the road scenario would be nothing of consequence happening, and best-case scenario would be ground breaking in the brain development and transplant field of medicine.

Travis Adamson felt like a man freed from a prison cell. As great as the set up at St. Mary's hospital had been, he was overjoyed when the warm summer breeze and bright sun hit his face. The dark luxury sedan headed north out of town and Emma Harris found herself watching his face and his reactions more than her driving as they passed from the city limits to the countryside. Travis' eyes were darting from one side of the road to the other and within two miles his mind was racing and retrieving information so quickly that he could barely contain himself in the seat next to the doctor.

"That's Roy Wilson's place…he drinks too damn much and is a wife beater. I feel so sorry for Dora, she's such a nice lady. We see her at the winery a lot, she drinks too much also but she has a reason, being married to that moron and all."

Emma was surprised by the sudden tirade that Travis was on; he sounded like a mid-fifties man, not a teenager. She stayed quiet and let him pour out every memory he could muster.

"He's going to lose that farm, there is no way he will make the payments and he's behind on his leased machinery. Bill Applebaum over at the bank is going to close his loans and repo the property and machinery."

Emma chose to gently interrupt the tirade for a moment.

"How do you know that, Travis?"

The young man in the seat next to her gave her a quizzical look.

"Travis, who's Travis? My name is Bruce, you know that Doc!"

This drew an equally quizzical look from the doctor. *"He's regressed into the transplant brain...he is remembering his old stomping grounds...interesting!"*

"I'm sorry, Bruce, please continue."

The young man's eyes were wide as if he were re-entering his world after a long absence.

"Jeez, what happened to the Harper place…it should be right there." He turned to the doctor for an answer and she just shrugged, having never heard of the family or place.

"Everything looks so different along here. What happened?" he asked again.

The doctor just shrugged and gave a gentle reply, hoping to settle her patient down.

"I have no idea, Bruce. I haven't lived here very long."

He just shook his head in a manner that looked like he was forcing information to come out. It seemed like the young man was fighting to retrieve his past life and his brain was not cooperating.

They rounded a curve in the countryside and passed a small cemetary on the right, overlooking a small village and crystal blue lake. Emma checked her passenger, waiting for a reaction; his corpse was buried here. The brain didn't register a thing, the passenger barely gave it a look.

They continued around a curve to the right and descended gradually toward the little white roadside store. Emma pulled up to the pumps in front and got out to refill her auto. Travis was out the door and up the wooden steps to the porch before she realized what was happening.

He opened the screen door to a world that he thought he would recognize. The layout was the same, the oldness of over a century of business hung in the air and on the walls;

pictures of people one hundred years before and fish caught from excursions long past. He picked up the scent of the aged store with an inhale and noted that it was just like yesterday.

"Where's Pete?" he asked the young cashier.

"Pete who?" she replied with a look of confusion.

"Pete...you know...Pete the owner." he replied with a touch of frustration in his voice.

"I'm sorry, sir. I've never heard of a guy named Pete. My dad owns this place...I'm stuck here today 'cuz he's sick."

Emma came through the screen door at this point, wondering what trouble she was walking into.

"No. Pete owns the store." Travis continued, looking toward the back room where the owner used to hang out. "He's usually here. Medium height, thin, dark hair, glasses on some days...you know, Pete!"

He was getting frustrated and he was suddenly confused as to how someone who was standing here yesterday seemed to no longer exist. The teen was worried and she looked for a way to avert trouble.

"Let me call my dad, he might know what you are talking about."

The young lady picked up her cell phone, punched a couple of keys, and was talking to her father, the store owner within fifteen seconds.

"Dad, there is a guy here looking for a Pete…someone named Pete…he says he owns our store." Words were exchanged and after a minute she put the phone down.

"My dad says that a guy named Pete used to own the store, but he sold it to us and he's gone…sorry."

Travis' face took on an expression that can only be described as weird. He was trying to process what he had just heard and was totally lost in confusion.

"But he was here yesterday…" was all he could murmur.

Emma stepped in and placed her index finger on the pad to be scanned, paying for her purchase. She took Travis gently by the arm to sooth him and they walked through the screen door and back onto the wooden porch.

"Let's get back in the car and I will try to explain it to you. We need to go to one other place first, ok?"

He moved slowly toward the car shaking his head, looking back every few feet in bewilderment. The doctor knew where they were going next and she was suddenly apprehensive. *Is this going to be too much?*

She piloted the sedan out of the drive area and back onto the road, taking a quick right to continue around the lake.

As she moved past a small dam on her right, Travis smiled and noted the water level pouring over the structure.

"He's smiling…this is good. He's recognizing home now." She continued past a small winery, toward a much larger church structure, and that's when everything fell apart.

"Shouldn't you slow down and turn up here?" he asked with a bit of an exclamation, wondering if she was suddenly lost.

"No, we are going to continue on." Suddenly he grasped at the dash and let out a scream.

"NO! NO! IT WON'T STOP…WHAT THE HELL!"

He was frantic as he grabbed an imaginary steering wheel in front of him and pounded the floor with his foot. There was no foot pedal to hit and stop but he was oblivious, lost in another world, another memory. Travis suddenly grabbed the wheel in front of Emma and began jerking it.

The doctor screamed now as the car, not moving more than twenty miles an hour suddenly veered toward the shoulder and oncoming trees. They were headed into the curve; the curve that had killed Bruce Nickel.

Chapter Eight

Emma regained control of the car, slamming on the brakes just before they left the shoulder and roadway. She was visibly shaking and stunned, vomit had reached her throat and the adrenaline was now surging through her body.

"DAMN IT, TRAVIS! WHAT IN THE WORLD DID YOU DO THAT FOR?"

The young man in the passenger seat had collapsed against the window and was crying, his body convulsing. He was omitting a shrieking sound that Emma had never heard before. *"This is not good."* was all she could mutter to herself, trying to calm her nerves as well.

She did a quick U turn and pulled into the church parking lot a couple of hundred yards away. Travis continued to cry, lost in his memory and unable to come back to the present. She leaned over to comfort him and he flung open the car door. After running about twenty feet, he stopped and screamed back at her.

"I'M DEAD, DON'T YOU SEE IT... I'M DEAD!"

He dropped to his knees on the dirt parking lot and then fell back to a seated position. "I'm dead. I'm dead. I'm dead."

The doctor moved to him slowly, not wanting to startle him or make him violent.

"Can I sit with you?" she whispered.

Travis looked up at her and nodded. They sat in an eerie silence, the warm sun beating down on them as midday approached. A car moved past on the road, taking the curve with little caution. Birds chirped and a boat motor hummed somewhere in the distance. She carefully put her arm around the young man and he melted into her, tears coming out again.

"I'm so sorry, Bruce." she whispered as she gently patted his back and held him.

"It wasn't my time to go. There was so much more to do." he responded quietly between sobs.

Her heart gave way and tears rolled gently down her cheeks as she held him a little tighter.

"Don't worry, you have a second chance now...I'm here for you."

A better part of an hour passed with them just sitting in the parking lot, much of the time quietly. He asked about the accident and she pushed him away from the topic as quickly as she could, not wanting to make him more upset.

"We can talk about all of that later. Let's get you back to the car and back to your room where you can cool off and relax. I will explain all of it later, ok?"

Travis nodded and they made their way back to Twin Lakes and the quiet refuge of his hospital room.

****

The celebrity patient was only supposed to stay in the northland for a week but on the sixth day he disappeared from the hospital. Travis had waited for the nurse to make her early morning rounds and then he casually slipped out of his room and down the hall. The gaggle of attendants were congregated around the station in the middle of the rooms and so he looked for a stairwell to leave through. It was easy to find and he was on the main level and walking out of the ambulance entrance before anyone gave him a second thought.

He had to get back, not only to the crash scene but to his house on the lake. He knew he would get all the answers he would need if he could just make his way back there. After the last episode the day before, it was pretty apparent that Dr. Harris would not take him back to his little town and so he had to get creative and find his way back.

Walking along the small side streets he came upon the local high school. As chance would have it, a pretty brunette was leaving the parking lot in her small, economy car.

Travis stuck out his thumb and smiled as he stood along the side of the street; she pulled over immediately and unlocked the door from the inside. Her window was already down and he stuck his head in.

"Hi, I'm Bruce...could I bum a ride off of you?" She returned his smile and was mesmerized with his good looks.

"I'm Kim, jump in. Where are you headed?" He slid into the car and played the situation for all it was worth.

"I'm going to Richwood. You wouldn't happen to be going that way, would you?" She grinned and let out a cute chuckle.

"I'm going anywhere but here...it's too nice to be in school." The escapee was warming up to her quickly; she was very attractive and her personality was radiant.

"Skipping school, huh. Shame on you!" he joked back, keeping the conversation alive. She was enjoying the playful interaction and replied with flirtation.

"You seem to be cutting out too! I've never seen you before...who's class are you skipping?"

He sat in the passenger seat and gave off the kind of confidence that young women always find attractive.

"I am new around here. Came up from the Cities. I start next week…just moving in this week." She beamed even more and shot him an attractive glance.

"So, where is your house?" He stumbled in his mind for a moment and then recalled an address from somewhere deep in his mind.

"North Buffalo Lake road…big house. My dad just retired."

The conversation continued in a flirtatious manner as they headed north out of town and somewhere along the line something changed. Travis was suddenly wanting to ask her out to a movie or a date of some kind; he was caught up in her. He was a sixteen-year old kid who wanted to hang out with her and hopefully do more than just hang out.

As they motored out through the countryside he became lost in his surroundings and when she approached the little white store he asked her to pull over and let him out.

"Well, Kim, I really hope to see you around." he purred with a smile. She reached across the seat and through the window, giving him her cell phone.

"Punch your number in and I will give you a call."

He frowned for a moment, lost in what to do next as he had no phone.

"My service doesn't work, my mom grounded me and turned it off. Can I write your number on my arm?"

She laughed as she locked eyes with him; she really wanted his number. He ran into the small store, grabbed a pen from the counter, and within a minute had a number to his new girlfriend written on his arm. It was so good to be young again!

Kim pulled out of the store lot, squealing her tires as she hit the pavement, and in a moment was gone. Travis hoped she wasn't gone for good. He watched with intrigue as her car disappeared and he realized he was suddenly very hungry.

He moved back into the store and slowly perused the narrow aisles. When the grumpy man behind the counter wasn't looking he slipped a couple of Snickers bars into his pocket. He moved back to the front of the store.

"Sir, I'm looking for the Nickel place…ever hear of it?" The man loosened up behind the counter, realizing the young man was friendly.

"Lived up on North Buffalo road…car accident, he's been gone for over a year. You familiar with the area?" Travis nodded confidently. "Why you lookin' for this Nickel guy?"

Travis shrugged as he slowly moved to the door and out of the conversation.

"He's an old relative of my dad's...I was told that if I was ever around here I should look him up."

Before he could get a response from the proprietor he moved through the screen door and back into the sunshine. He had somewhere to go.

Travis walked out to the pumps and surveyed the scene. He knew this little town well and he made his way around the corner and onto the shoulder of County Road 34. The young man walked slowly, hesitant, not knowing exactly why he had to come back to this area. He strode in the warm sun past the small dam that turned the lake into a river and he listened to the birds singing and insects buzzing.

The soft smile left Travis' face as he walked past the quiet vineyard and winery and continued to the large church; he had his emotional breakdown here the day before. Instead of walking over to the curve where he lost his life, he turned to the right and walked down North Buffalo Road to his old house.

The large, light blue house trimmed in white had once been small but had been added onto multiple times to create quite a massive sight. The yard was neatly kept and the circular drive was inviting with all of its plants and décor. He stopped and looked over the house and property from a distance; no one seemed to be home.

Approaching with caution, he checked the road in both directions to make sure no one saw him. Neighbors in this area were nosy, they would stop and question almost anyone they did not know. Being a teen, he was more vulnerable as adults would wonder what his purpose was and why he wasn't in school.

Travis casually walked along the circle to the front door and peered inside, acting as if he was about to ring the bell. Everything was quiet and still.

"Will she recognize me? Of course not, I look like a sixteen-year old kid...ha, ha, ha."

A car rumbled down the dirt road and Travis felt the sudden urge to bolt around the side of the house toward a small, wooded camping area. He dodged behind a large oak tree as the squad car pulled into the circle and an officer got out. The cop made his way up to the garage entrance, moving too close for the young man's comfort, and then went inside.

"I wonder what that is about? Law enforcement in my house?"

He sat still, watching the doorway and then he heard the deck door on the back of the house close with a bang. He moved silently down the tree line and toward the back of the structure and the lake.

"There she is. Damn, she looks a little older, but she still has that body..."

The sixteen-year old brain took over and he pondered all of the fun things he could do with her and then the old man's brain reappeared. He quickly realized that she was mostly all show and no go, that it wouldn't be worth the effort.

The sheriff moved down to the boat landing where she was standing and, when he jumped up on the slight incline, she gave him a long kiss.

"Hmm, lovers huh? Didn't take her long to get over me."

He felt a sense of rage boiling up inside him and then the young man suddenly reasoned things out.

"A woman who looks like that would never want a kid like me. Kim, on the other hand..."

He smiled to himself as he watched the scene from afar, becoming more and more confused by the moment. His brain began to hurt, he suddenly felt very tired.

Travis moved out to the edge of the woods and crossed the dusty road carefully. He then wound his way through a large field to a stand of tall pines and a cool bay on the other side. He followed the bay to the lake, as he had many times in the past, and he settled underneath a huge tree that reached out over the water. Sitting with his back against the large trunk, he looked out over the water and opened one of the candy bars from his pocket. It was devoured in a matter of a minute, the wrapper tucked into his pocket, and he dozed off amid the cool breeze from the lake.

"The wonderful smell of the lake."

He was dreaming now and the phrase kept running through his mind. He felt like he was somewhat awake yet asleep at the same time. The pleasant sounds coming from the water and the wooded area around him were present in his consciousness, yet he was floating in a surreal manner.

"My beautiful, blue boat."

Bruce was on his boat with his business partner Ed, and they were fishing thirty yards off shore, looking at the majestic oak that reached out from shore toward them. The fishing lines were in the water, the boat was swaying gently, and the cold beers tasted really good.

"You know, Ed, you are my best friend in the whole world. It's been quite a journey with the firm, hasn't it? I've been thinking that maybe it's time to get out, to retire to this place permanently. What do you think?"

He friend looked across the boat at him, slightly stunned but not totally surprised. The boss had been coming in fewer times during the week and late arrivals had become the norm. This announcement still caught Ed a bit off guard.

"Brucie, you couldn't leave our firm if you wanted to. There is too much to do and we still need you...how about just cutting back on hours? Besides, that hottie of yours needs all the money you can provide, she's high maintenance!" Both men chuckled at the comment and took another swig of their beers.

"Damn, she does look good, doesn't she?" the old man responded with pride and virility, happy to have her as his trophy wife.

Chapter Nine

Dr. Harris made her way out of the hospital cafeteria and down the hall to the elevator bank. It was time to make her rounds and she had Travis on her mind; the events of the day before had shocked and scared her.

"This could be a permanent setback in our progress...I wonder how he slept last night?"

She had desired to make a visit earlier but her morning became increasingly hectic at the harvest center and Seth couldn't handle the work alone. Lunch was a quick sandwich and a Diet Sprite before she got back into her rounds.

No one had a clue, the duty nurses were busy with a famous local who had suffered a heart attack on the tennis court that morning. Not a single nurse had bothered to check on the young man in their care; they had no cause to be concerned because he spent his days playing video games and going out for drives with the doctor. In reality it had only been one drive, but they were careless and unconcerned. The local celebrity was a bigger deal in their world.

Emma peaked her head around the corner of the doorway, curious to see what the young patient was up to.

"Has anyone seen Travis this morning?" she called back to the nurses' station in a voice with a tone not appropriate for the ICU.

"No, Doctor Harris.   We had a busy morning, here...wasn't he with you?"

Panic took hold of her mind and she moved quickly toward the elevator bank.   Descending two floors, she entered the main lobby and scanned the waiting area.

"Maybe the kid just needed some fresh air and a change of scenery."

He was nowhere to be found, the lobby was empty accept for the admitting clerk behind her desk.

"You didn't happen to see a boy, a teenager come through here, did you?"

The young lady behind the counter shook her head back and forth, giving a definitive answer. Emma went through the front doors to the parking lot and hopped into her sedan. She quickly scanned the premises and then it occurred to her. She took off for Richwood Road.

The vehicle slowed as she neared the crash scene from the seemingly distant past. There were no visible signs that anyone had perished other than a small, floral roadside memorial hanging on a sign. Few people remembered the tragedy. She doubled back to the church parking lot, scanning carefully and saw no one of interest. Down the dirt road toward the lake, around a curve, and past the big blue house. No sign of him.

"Where in the world are you, kid?" she thought out loud, frustration overtaking her senses.

"This is bad, this is bad...this is REALLY BAD!" she screamed inside the airconditioned interior as she passed more lake homes and cabins to the east.

The road came to an end, a chain and a NO TRESPASSING sign closed her off from the wooded point. Then he appeared and stopped suddenly in surprise. His shocked expression turned to a silly grin as he continued toward the car. His boyish gait suddenly got really sheepish as he walked around to the passenger side and opened the door.

"Going my way?" he said tentatively while trying to win her over with his smile. She blew up.

"What in the hell do you think you are doing?! SERIOUSLY, what are you thinking?!"

He leaned away from her and rolled his eyes like a typical teenager.

"Whoa, don't have a heart attack now...settle down." She turned a burning look at him.

"Don't you tell me to settle down, young man. You pulled a stupid stunt that could have killed you." Her voice sounded more like a concerned mother than Dr. Emma Harris.

Travis was scared now; he hadn't thought of any possible medical concerns. He was thinking like teenagers think, that he was invincible. He didn't say a thing while the doctor turned the car around and headed back toward the church. As they approached the blue house Travis spoke up. The squad car was gone.

"There was my home...one of the nicest on the lake." He said it quietly, wondering how it could all be gone from his life...how his life could be over.

"My, it's beautiful Bruce. I'm sorry."

The young patient turned to her and quietly requested "Please don't call me Bruce anymore. I'm Travis from now on."

She didn't know how to react and so she kept on driving slowly past the home and lakeshore. Travis turned around and looked out the back window, hoping to catch another glimpse of Faith by the water. There was nobody down below, the dock and pontoon appeared empty.

"Say, doc...would there be any reason why the sheriff would have pulled up to the house back there? He seemed awfully friendly with the lady who lives there."

She pulled onto County 34 and continued back to town, his little escape stunt still stinging in her mind a bit.

"I don't know. I have no idea about who lives there now. I don't get out here much, except with you. Maybe the sheriff is related to them or lives there or something. I don't know."

They drove on in silence for another five minutes before Travis returned to the subject.

"How could I find out what happened to my…I mean Bruce's wife after I…I mean Bruce, died?"

She thought quietly as she drove on for a bit, not real sure herself as this was not her expertise. Encouragement in this endeavor could be a bad idea and so staying silent was, in her judgement, the best course. The quiet tension in the car seemed like a childhood game and she broke first.

"I suppose you check the library or historical society in town and try to find records of the crash. Then an obituary. Then maybe talk to some residents around here and see if they can give you any information. Did Bruce have any close friends here? Maybe check with them?"

The young man turned his gaze from the outside to her and smiled.

"Those are good ideas. Thanks, doc. Hey, you think you could help me?"

He pulled another Snickers bar from his pocket and took a big bite. She looked at him, then the bar, then him again.

"I don't want to know...don't want to know."

He shot her his charming smile while chewing, let out a light laugh, and took another big bite.

Dr. Harris covered for Travis' absence with the nurses as best as she could but there was still hell to pay with the morning staff; they had figured out the real story. Using his best charm, he soon won the group over and was enjoying the attention of his last night in the hospital.

Tomorrow he would be driven back to the University Hospital by the doctor for one last night's stay and then he would check out and travel with his mother back to Iowa. Travis was not looking forward to going back home; he really wanted to stay up north and find the pretty girl who gave him a ride out of town.

He had Kim's number on his arm, but he was a chicken when it came to girls. If he could be Bruce he wouldn't have any problem, but he couldn't just turn on one brain and then another at his will; everything just happened on its own.

"Even if I call her, I don't know what to say...what do I do? Invite her to visit in the hospital? Creepy..."

He vowed to himself to call her in the future, but when he would act on this would remain uncertain. He drifted off to sleep with the ten o'clock news on the television.

****

"Geez Ed, can you tell Darrell to get up here on the double? We haven't got all day!"

The boardroom was paneled in a dark, expensive looking wood and the chairs were highbacked leather; the place felt important. A short, balding man with dark rimmed glasses almost fell through the huge, double doors as he entered the meeting space. Ed moved quietly behind him, chuckling softly.

"Sorry Bruce, had to take the call. Witherspoon over at First National was wondering if we wanted to handle some more of their cashless stock option work…particularly with Delta Airlines. They have a bit of a mess over their right now with the Dave Allen thing going on. They say he might be in court as early as next week."

The smallish man was talking a mile a minute, nervous over keeping the boss waiting.

"You know, Allen could be going away. What a moron, I mean really? Shuffling money overseas…direct to accounts? He looks like a damn drug dealer, you know?"

Bruce was sitting at the head of the table, spewing out condemnation with disgust. Ed piped in, following his boss' lead.

"I hope you said yes to the offer! The commission could be really good and our new account numbers would jump as well. What did you say?"

A strange vibration entered his dream and caused him to be confused. There was a siren off in the distance and he heard a door slam and people running. He couldn't see a thing though, except for Ed and Darrell sitting on each side of him. He drifted back as Bruce spoke up.

"There is something that I think you should know...I have already talked to Ed on this and we are not in agreement." Darrell fell silent, waiting for a big news drop...the kind that made for great gossip.

"I am not going to leave the firm until late next year at the earliest, I think there is too much to do and the markets are unstable." The news WAS big, as Darrell had no idea that Bruce was pondering retirement.

"Ed here thinks that I should take off now. He says it's..."

Ed shifted forward in his chair and interrupted the boss.

"It is better to get out while you still have your health and the markets are good. The longer you stay around, the more tenuous things could get... in so many ways! I have everything covered here and you will still be pulling a share of the commissions...our stock value is good also. There is really no reason to stay...run up north to that hot wife of yours and enjoy life, buddy!" Darrell noticed an uneasiness in the boss' attitude and demeanor.

The boss swiveled his chair slowly toward the third man in rank and smiled quietly, studying the discomfort that the little man was showing.

"Eddie wants Senior Partner...the best take of commissions!"

He turned to his best friend and the two of them laughed, knowing that it was at least partly true.

"What do you think, Darrell?"

The little man dropped his head and looked at the table top, beads of sweat forming on his shiny forehead.

"I don't know, Bruce. I do not specialize in this kind of stuff...I'm all about the books, the numbers." He spoke quietly, a tinge of fear in his response. Bruce was in no mood to deal with a waffling employee.

"For crise sakes Darrell, what would you DO?"

This was a losing proposition; either tick off the boss or the second man in charge. The safest play was to side with Bruce.

"Well then, I guess I would stick it out and keep going. If you like your job, why would you quit?" He paused and avoided looking into the eyes of both men.

"I think you should stay."

Ed, sitting directly across from the timid man, shot him a look of death.

Travis shivered awake in the darkness of the silent hospital suite. It took him a moment to reacclimate himself; the image of Ed's scary expression was still burned into his brain.

"God, sometimes it sucks to be Bruce." he muttered aloud, the sound echoing in the quiet room.

The sleepy boy turned over and looked at the window, following the rays from the moon that shone across his floor and walls. Travis found his Styrofoam cup of ice water on the bed stand and took a long drag through the plastic straw before he set it back down and rolled over. He was sleeping again within a minute.

Chapter Ten

The doctor sat in her office with a recorder in one hand and the other slowly working its way through her short, blonde hair. She hated case notes, they were a nuisance that she could live without. These seemed more important than normal though, they were about Travis Adamson and his transformation over the last three months. Dr. Stuart walked up to her office doorway and stared with curiosity; she waved him in as she continued to talk to the recorder.

Stuart closed the door gently behind him and sat down in one of her leather side chairs to listen in. After about three more minutes of an analysis, she clicked off the little device and the guest broke in with questions.

"I heard you say that Travis is drifting between both brains, is that to be expected at this point?"

The lead doctor placed the small, gray recorder carefully on the desk in front of her and hooked it up to her computer to run a transfer. She folded her hands delicately in front of her as she pondered the vast situation, a new situation for her to deal with.

"I don't know if 'normal' is the right term...every one of these cases is so different. I wouldn't think of anything really as 'normal' yet. He is moving between the transplanted brain of Bruce and his own section…the Travis brain."

She stopped for a moment and thought about how to describe the next series of events without sounding ridiculous.

"There is something else taking place in Travis' case though, something we have not seen before."

"Because Bruce Nickel, the transplant, was so much older we seem to have the patient drifting through a series of years in a dreamlike state. He keeps dreaming about random events in Bruce's life, but at vastly different periods. I can't really put a timeline together to define what he is recalling."

Dr. Stuart was working through the scenario in his mind with interest. Both professionals sat silently for a bit, pondering the situation.

"So, you have no idea of what era of time the dreams are coming from? Are they taking place in the same place, so to speak? Same people? Is there any specific thing that triggers the dreams to occur?"

Emma paused to reflect and consider these ideas more fully.

"I really haven't a clue…I guess I never thought about the dreams in that way. I have been trying to solve a mystery of sorts instead and so I have been looking at the dreams as you would look at a movie...looking for clues."

Stuart was engaged in the process and he was always fond of a good mystery.

"Let's talk to the kid...maybe a little later today? I haven't seen him in a while...it will be good."

The lead doctor smiled at him and described the complexity of the situation.

"The kid is back in Iowa, back home with mom. He started school last week. I spoke with both of them on the phone last night and it sounds like he is off to a rough start. Other than one friend of his, it seems like many of the kids are having fun treating him like a freak. He is not happy...poor kid."

Stuart felt sorry for Travis; he could relate because he had once been the target of the popular kids. Some of those kids were now sweeping floors and mopping up puke in the hospitals that he worked in. Vengeance can be satisfying, he thought to himself.

"Can we get him up here to attend school and work with us for an extended period of time? Say a month or two?"

Emma worked through the possibility and then made a better suggestion.

"What if we take Travis back up to Twin Lakes and enroll him up there. Mom can come with…last I checked she was cleaning houses in and around Waterloo. We can find her a job and apartment or small house up there. Then we can really study him and immerse him in the area that he seems so fixated on. I would bet that a lot of memories would come back if he kept moving throughout a familiar area."

****

Using some of her best salesmanship skills, Dr. Harris convinced the Adamsons to move north for the school year. Somewhere, deep down in her mind, she had a desire to solve the mystery of Bruce Nickel and see Travis Adamson shine in life. Travis had the same desire. The doctor worked hard to set everything up and the family headed north to a new beginning.

Emma worked hard to set the family up right because she also felt a sympathy for the hard life that they had endured. The medical bills had piled up and the church and community had raised a ton of money to pay off the big expenses, but the doctor knew that they were struggling to make it each day.

Sylvia found a day job working as a lunch lady at the elementary school in town and also worked cleaning the organ harvesting lab twice a week at night. Travis started his junior year at the high school on the first week of October. He was happy.

He knew her the minute he saw her, even though he was behind her. She was walking with two friends toward the cafeteria when he piped up from over her shoulder. He felt a little like Bruce, a little brave.

"Hey Beautiful. Yeah, You." She spun around, her long black hair flailing over her shoulders.

"It's you!"

Her friends turned with stunned looks, from him to her and back again.

"I didn't think I would see YOU again...you didn't call me!" Now she had a bit of a scowl and he knew he had to think fast.

"Well, you see..." he stated, turning on the charm with his smile, "I had a secret mission to complete for the CIA...if I would have called you it would have blown my cover. Could've gotten you killed, you know?"

She laughed graciously, enjoying the attention she was getting in front of her friends. Introductions were made among the group and he sat with the group at lunch. It felt good to get to know her, she had been on his mind for quite a while.

"When we get a chance to be alone, I can tell you more about why I couldn't get in touch with you...I really wanted to talk to you."

She smiled and it made him giddy. "I wanted to talk to you too."

Chapter Eleven

"Come on, Doc. I REALLY want to play football...I will be careful!" She looked across the table at him with a stare that was nothing short of incredulous.

"Are you out of your freaking mind?!" He sunk back a little and she leaned toward him.

"You could DIE! If you think I will give consent for this...this sport...this...you've GOT TO BE KIDDING!"

He tilted his head to one side and tried to play it cool.

"You only live once, Doc. Bruce was an All-American...I could be too!"

She settled her temper and mind down a bit and leaned back in her chair. Her head moved slowly, back and forth. Emma felt sorry for the young man, she knew that his life would never be like a normal kid's life. There were always precautions to take, things to be missed.

"I can't let you do it. Think about it...one strong hit to the head, a concussion follows...a brain bruise. It could permanently set you back, not temporarily, but permanently. Your brain is still adapting to the splice, at the very minimum you wouldn't be ready for anything involving contact until your senior year."

He had tried his best, but common sense won out. He really wanted to play, to be someone important, to impress Kim. It was hopeless, at least for two years, maybe forever. Doctor Harris wouldn't give the consent and his mom wouldn't sign the papers without her blessing. No paperwork, no play…that simple. He was brooding in front of the doctor now, working for a little sympathy. She changed the subject with hopes of lightening the mood.

"So, tell me, have you found anything more on Bruce or Ed?"

"I haven't." he replied sheepishly.

In truth, he had been spending a lot of time chasing Kim and they were becoming a 'thing' at school. He also hit it off with a kid named Danny Lewis in his math class and they found they had a lot in common, including living two houses away from each other.

"Are you busy with school?" Dr. Emma inquired, curious as to what he was up to.

"You could say that." he said with a smile. "I have a girlfriend."

Dr. Harris returned his smile; she knew it was only a matter of time and she felt this was good for his progress. He was miles ahead in a social sense of where he had ever been before. The transplant was working. Travis Adamson was well on his way to leading the life of a normal teenage boy.

"A girlfriend, huh?" she chuckled as she studied his face, noticing a slight blush. "Is she cute?"

His smile grew in intensity.

"Of course. I only date hot girls."

She laughed now. "You haven't dated anyone yet!"

He retorted "Well, I'm one for one then. I have impeccably high standards."

The doctor loved the fact that they could have this rapport. A year ago the young man was unable to speak at this intellectual level; everything he said was in the most simple of sentences. *"Impeccably...impressive use of words!"*

"Tell me about her...who is she?"

Travis was uncomfortable now because he was just learning about Kim himself and was unsure of the status of their relationship.

"Well, I met her a couple of weeks ago at school…her name is Kim. She's really cute and funny." He trusted Emma enough to continue.

"We like to hang out together, along with Danny, at lunch and between classes. I like her a lot."

He stopped here, hoping the topic would change and become more comfortable.

"Have you had any more dreams?" the doctor continued, noting the uncomfortable posture that had suddenly taken over.

"No. Nothing really. My brain has been very quiet. Is that normal?"

Doctor Harris tried her best to calm his worries.

"That is very normal. The brain takes time to adapt and adjust to your body. You are progressing very well, in a series of stages, and now your new brain is growing together with the splice of your old one. Just wait, your brain will get very active again when it is ready. You are doing very well, Travis, and I am so proud of you."

The young man beamed with pride.

****

"Uh, 4649?"

Travis blurted out with a high pitched, nervous squeak after what seemed like a lifetime of silence. The class broke into laughter and he turned to his friend, Danny, with a horrified look on his face.

"Trav…" the friend whispered back. "It's the square root of 8."

The embarrassed young man surveyed the class in a hurry and composed himself.

"Mr. Tretvin, I believe the correct answer is Square Root of Eight."

He said it with confidence and nodded to his best friend, receiving a smile in return. The elderly, thin teacher at the front nodded with a chuckle. "Thank you for the right answer…you had me really worried for a moment!"

"Geez, Trav, what was THAT all about?" the friend and confidant asked when they walked out of the classroom at the end of the hour.

"I have no idea…kind of weird, huh? I keep seeing this number in my head. 4649, over and over…then I see this large, red, plastic container…it's dark in there…in the room, but not too dark. It keeps going through my head, over and over."

Danny turned to his friend with a worried expression and stopped walking.

"Are you going to be OK?"

Travis nodded with a smile and stated "Don't worry, pal. My doctor says this is all normal and good."

The duo headed to the cafeteria and met up with Kim and her friends after grabbing trays and piling on food. Everyone was seated in the bright lunch room and the chatter was at a high volume.

"Are you going to eat that?" Travis turned as he pointed at Kim's tray.

"No way…its mystery meat. No one here knows what it is. I think the dark lines are tire tracks…must be road kill!"

Their end of the table laughed at her joke and Travis used his plastic fork to help himself to the brown circular slab of meat.

"You're really going to eat that?" she exclaimed with mock horror. He smiled and kissed her quickly on the cheek while Danny looked on with a bit of jealousy. She grinned and he explained his logic.

"I'm a growing boy. This mystery is really 'Mister Rib'…it's nothing more than a pork patty dunked in barbeque sauce…Mmmm… so good."

With that explanation he and Danny tapped their mystery steaks together, took a big bite each, and smiled triumphantly. Everyone groaned in unison.

Travis moved his conversation across the table to his friend.

"What do you think 4649 is?"

Danny stopped mid-bite and placed the pork slab back onto the plate.

"I don't know. It's possibly a combination to a lock, but not a rotary one like the kind on our lockers. A bike lock maybe, where the numbers line up?" They both sat quietly for a moment and pondered the numbers. "Maybe it's an address?"

"Could be." Travis replied with some confidence. "That would make sense. Do you know any areas around here where there are four digit addresses?"

Danny sat in thought for a moment, a shrug overtaking his shoulders.

"Would have to be a fire post, the numbers in town all seem to be three digits, you know. Like ours...832 and 844...all three digit numbers. The fire tags out in the rural areas have five or six, but there might be some with four."

The best friend sensed the confusion on his new friend's face and proceeded to explain it further for him.

"You know out by the lakes? The cabins? They all have those posts with red numbers bolted onto them? That's their addresses...fire tags for the fire department. The lots have long numbers that the emergency vehicles can use to find them on 911 calls."

Travis nodded, understanding everything now.

"Should we look for four- digit numbers then?" Danny nodded back.

"Sounds like a good place to start."

****

The rookie teacher was walking down the hall, aware of all the young men staring at her. She was used to the attention, four and a half years of college consisted of men trying to win her over. These were young men, kids, and even though she was only five years older it was still so strange to ponder what was running through their minds. She didn't have to guess, she knew.

Travis saw her walking towards him and he pulled Danny toward the lockers along the wall.

"Who in the world is that?" he whispered with emphasis.

"I don't know. She's new here. Smoking HOT!"

Dan suddenly turned to his friend and began to worry immediately.

"Oh, no…Trav, you got that look…what are you going to do?"

Travis was beaming at the young teacher as she walked by; to her he was just another boy. Their eyes met for a moment and they exchanged smiles. He moved in a few paces behind her and followed her up the stairwell.

"Wow! Teachers are sure different today than when I went to school. Look at that…damn!"

Travis' eyes were focused on her backside as she moved up the steps and he was lost in infatuation. She reached the top, turned into the wide hallway, and walked to the first classroom to her left. He kept following and Danny was panicking behind him.

They stopped outside the open door that she had entered. The nameplate on the wall said Miss Weston.

"Trav! What the hell! What are we doing? What are you going to do?" the whispering was loud and Travis held his finger up to his lips to silence his friend.

"I'm going to go in and introduce myself. Then I am going to talk to her."

The look on the pursuers face was unfamiliar to his friend, and Dan suddenly knew that he was dealing with Bruce.

"Are you CRAZY?! What in the world would you say to her??" The young friend was scared of his buddy, knowing that this could go bad in a hurry.

"I will introduce myself, charm her with my good looks and personality, and then plant the hottest kiss on her she has ever had."

Danny immediately burst into uncontrolled laughter and quickly headed for the staircase.

"You are crazy, Travis Adamson, absolutely crazy."

He disappeared down the stairs and Travis followed, but not before reading the name plate on the classroom door one last time.

"*Miss Weston, hmmm.*"

Chapter Twelve

The mist was slowly burning off the surface of the lake as the small watercraft ran straight out from the dock. Most of the guests were not up yet, many had indulged in too much alcohol and casual drugs from the night before. Ed and Bruce were playing with their new toy, a remote-control device that you could connect to small cars and boats. Bruce had spent a small fortune on the toy, but later found it had a practical purpose as well. He could hook it up to his riding lawnmower, the most expensive one made, and he could move the expansive grass lot while sitting on his deck.

"This is the damnedest thing I have ever seen!" Ed chuckled, still intoxicated from the night before.

"I know, isn't it great?" the host replied with a bit of braggadocio as he watched his buddy run the small boat through its paces. "I got it at the State Fair, got a helluva deal on it. Then I rebuilt the whole thing, made it really work! Only twenty-five hundred."

Ed looked quickly at his friend and noted the wide smile.

"Only twenty-five hundred...you're funny, Bruce." The boat continued to do circles as it moved to the center of the lake.

****

Travis woke from the dream, feeling happy. As he figured out his surroundings on this sleepy November morning, he realized that it was Saturday and he rolled over to go back to sleep.

"Twenty-five hundred, twenty-five hundred..."

The number continued to float through his mind and he suddenly had a hankering for pancakes. His bare feet hit the cold, wooden floor and he grabbed for a pair of less than clean socks. After pulling them on and slipping on his bathrobe, he made his way downstairs to the kitchen.

The young man gazed out the window over the sink that looked into the back yard. A light snow was blanketing the ground and the air looked frigid. He turned toward the table in the nook when he heard a coffee cup return to the oak table.

"Good morning, Trav. Can I make you something for breakfast?" Sylvia was sitting alone, sipping the hot java, already dressed for the day.

"Umm…pancakes would be good." he replied hesitantly, not really remembering who she was.

Every day this lady would appear in his house and everyone said she was his mom, but for some crazy reason he did not believe it. He couldn't remember her.

"Shouldn't I be able to remember my mom?"

Ms. Adamson rose from her chair and began preparing breakfast for her son. A sadness overtook her at times like this. The transplant was a success and she knew that her son was beyond lucky to now be able and live a normal life.

The trade-off was what made her sad. Before the transplant her son knew who she was…his mom, Sylvia. Now he had no idea. He tried to fake it well on some days, but she knew better. Her boy was confused as to her identity.

The young man watched the squirrels in the back yard, fighting at the bird feeder as the snow picked up in intensity. Everything was a bright white and he shuddered while thinking about the outside temperature.

The pancakes kept coming and, after slathering each with butter and syrup, he was putting all of them away. With his eating habits of late, he would be an offensive lineman if he was allowed to play football. The young boy was filling out into a man quickly.

"Is it ok if I take Kim to the movies tonight?" he asked, hoping for a resounding yes.

"Of course. That would be fine. Will you need a drive to the theater?"

He didn't want to be treated like a junior high student.

"No. We can walk it or she can drive. Thanks though."

The doting mom felt deflated, like she was no longer needed in his life. He grew up so fast after the transplant.

Danny showed up as he was finishing his fifth pancake. Sylvia answered the front door and Travis could hear him tramping the snow off his feet before making his way back to the kitchen.

"Hey dreamer boy…how goes it?"

Sylvia offered the visitor a stack of pancakes and he accepted with an eager smile. She felt it would be best to leave the two high-schoolers on their own in the alcove.

"Any luck with 4649?" Travis asked, knowing that his friend had become fixated on the problem of the numbers.

"No luck. I checked the directory on the net. Nothing. Even went over to the firehouse and talked to Johnny Hawk. He looked in the station's directory and there is nothing with that number in Becker or Ottertail counties. It's not an address." Travis got up and put his empty plate and fork in the sink.

"Want to double date with Kim and me tonight? We're going to hit a movie."

Danny lifted a fork load of pancakes to his mouth, leaned back, and studied his friend. After chewing them up he replied in with a voice of mock surprise.

"And who am I going to go with? My right hand? I haven't dated ANYBODY...I'm not a stud like you."

Travis laughed lightly.

"I'm not a stud. Kim says that she thinks if you asked Susan Thompson she would go out with you."

Danny let out the laugh, louder than his friend.

"Susan Thompson? Are you kidding me? She's WAY out of my league!" He continued loudly. "If I was the only guy in the room she wouldn't notice me!"

Travis leaned back and surveyed his friend now.

"You know what your problem is?" He pointed across the table.

"You have no confidence. No confidence whatsoever. Kim asked her Wednesday what she thought of you. She said she thinks you are cute. You're nice. Think about it. She's almost best friends with Kim...it's a great deal for us. They already like each other so we don't have to deal with feuding girlfriends. It's a slam dunk. I'm going to call Kim and have her invite Susan."

Danny's expression turned to one of terror.

"Oh my God, don't you dare! I can't go out with her...I won't know what to say, what to do! Don't call her!" He was genuinely scared.

"Um, Dan, I don't know how to say this so I'll just say it. It's pretty much a done deal. I asked Kimmy yesterday and she said she'd talk to Sue. I'm just waiting to hear back. Kim's probably still asleep, but I will bet you a hundred bucks Susan says yes."

He smiled the widest smile toward his friend and began laughing as he thought he saw Danny sink down in his chair.

"You know, for a dude who's just gotten his brain transplanted, you sure seem to know one hell of a lot about women."

The transplantee just smiled.

"Bruce has been teaching me all kinds of things about women. You should be very jealous...I'm way ahead of my time!"

He just continued to wear the shit eating grin that drove Danny crazy. The single friend just sat back and shook his head, too worried to continue the conversation.

Kim called to confirm their date around lunch time and the boys spent the afternoon playing video games and talking about women, particularly sex. Danny had heard many things dating back to his junior high days, but this was an eye-opening education and he was pretty sure it would be a long, long time before he ever needed to put any of this information to use. He was absolutely thrilled, however, about one thing. Susan was going to be his date to the movies.

Chapter Thirteen

"Hey beautiful, did the money show up?" Edward Payne was putting on all of his charm. His girlfriend was about to become a very wealthy woman.

"Hi babe. The money hasn't come yet, but I think it should be here any day. My lawyer says it's just small details that are holding the settlement up. He says everything looks good."

The business man was calling his best friend's wife from an office tower in the Twin Cities. He had a lot more to do now that the controlling partner was no longer alive.

"I think I will be coming north for the weekend. I really miss you...will you be around?"

She hesitated, not knowing exactly how to give him the brush off. The silence told him more than he wanted to know.

"Faith, are you there?" She hesitated for a second and then came up with an excuse.

"I'm probably going to head over to Fargo. My dad is not doing so well, he's back in the hospital again. I think we will have to put things off for another week."

Ed's heart sank a bit. This wasn't a matter of a weekend of sex, he could have that with many different women that he knew. It was all about Faith. He had wanted her for years while she had been married to his best friend. Now she was his for the taking and it suddenly seemed so difficult.

"I get it, babe. You take all the time you need to see your dad. I can come up another weekend or maybe you can come down, right?" He didn't want to sound too desperate, but he really wanted to spend quality time with her.

"I knew you would understand. You're the best, Ed. I have to go, I'm in the middle of something important. I will call you later."

He disconnected the call and sat back in his office chair, wondering where the future would take the both of them. Faith put down her cell phone on the bed stand, pulled up the covers, and went back to dreaming about her cop boyfriend.

****

Spring was finally arriving and Travis had all A's on his report card. Kim's grades were steadily improving as she tried harder in school to impress her boyfriend. Prom was just around the corner, but none of the four were interested in spending all the money necessary to attend. Travis, Kim, Danny, and Susan would have to find something else to occupy their time, the big dance was out of the question.

The headaches started slowly, they weren't a big deal but just a bit of an inconvenience. The dreams came nightly now and the pictures in his head were becoming clearer. The '4649' dream hit him on a Thursday night and he knew he had to do something right away. Travis decided to skip school and take his friends with him for an adventure of sorts. It was time to solve a puzzle that had confounded him for way too long.

They cut out of school after third hour, knowing that they would miss only one full hour and then lunch. It was their best chance of not getting caught; not that it mattered much because Travis had quickly become a favorite among teachers and administration. Kim would probably face the most trouble as she had a past that was less than stellar when it came to attendance.

The foursome made their way out of the parking lot and out of town in Kim's small car.

"What exactly are we looking for?" Susan asked from the back seat, sitting a little too close to Danny and enjoying it.

"I don't know. I just have to see everything in my head. It's a round container, like the kind they keep coffee in. It's red. I don't know why it's important, I just know it is."

Susan looked at her boyfriend with a puzzled look and he returned the same expression with a shrug.

"What happens if we get caught?" Kim asked nervously.

"We're not going to get caught. If it looks dangerous, we won't go in. Just trust me on this."

The small car made the right hand turn at the little white store and continued up the hill toward the big church at the top. They took the right and started down the muddy road toward the lake. The big blue house was on their right and they drove past slowly, looking for any activity. They moved on to the next cabin on the road.

"Doesn't look like anybody's home. This is good, very good." Travis said quietly with anticipation. "Pull up in this driveway here. If anybody asks, we will tell them we are lost."

Kim piloted the car into the narrow asphalt drive and they all got out. Following Travis, they made their way through the damp landscape and heavily wooded area to the edge of the lakeside property.

There it stood in quiet beauty; Bruce's old lake home. Travis led the quartet across the lawn slowly, surveying the scene for anyone or anything that might be a threat. He approached the front porch, walked up the wooden steps, and quietly knocked on the white paneled door.

"What in the hell are you doing?" Danny asked in alarm.

"Just follow my lead." He responded as the three sidekicks were in a state of fright.

There was no answer. After knocking a little louder and waiting for minute, no one showed up and so they walked around the back of the residence. Travis led the way and he moved a large, white, plaster planter to expose a key to the back door.

"Ah, still where I left it." He said quietly with a nostalgic smile. The three friends exchanged puzzled glances.

He slid the key into the lock and turned the handle to open the door.

"C'mon In!" he blurted with humor.

"Are you kidding? If we get caught we are all going to jail! Breaking and entering...ever hear of it!" Danny was freaking out and the girls didn't know what to do.

"We are not going to get caught. Just stay quiet and don't mess anything up. She will never know. Stay here if you want, but I'm going in to find the red can."

"She? Who is SHE?" Kim asked in a whisper as they were about to enter.

"Someone I used to know... not a big deal." Travis responded, not wanting anyone to pursue the topic further. Kim would freak out if she knew he was Bruce and had been married to the blond bombshell that everyone knew as Faith.

Taking care to make sure that their shoes were clean, they walked into the house and quietly made their way to the kitchen. They started opening cabinets, looking for the red container.

"Found it." Susan whispered as she grabbed the Folger's coffee can from next to the coffee pot.

"You don't have to whisper, there is no one here." Travis offered, hoping to put his friends at ease.

Susan handed the can to Travis and he opened it slowly, taking care to not spill any of the contents on the floor. The last thing they needed was to clean up a mess.

"Nothing but coffee…keep looking."

They searched high and low throughout the house and Travis spent a lot of time admiring the things that Bruce had collected and displayed. From sports memorabilia to fishing mounts and even a golf trophy or two, he was fascinated by what his predecessor had accomplished. *And he even had a trophy wife. Nice work, Bruce!*

The four students were somewhat dejected by the time they had finished moving through the house. Danny and Susan moved out to the back deck that overlooked the lake, waiting for their friends.

"One more place to check. The garage."

Travis and Kim moved from the laundry area into the triple garage, turning on lights that seemed way too dim. As he moved around the scene it all came back to him.

"This is it. It's here." A quiet pause.

"What's here?" she answered quietly.

"It's here, I know it."

He spun suddenly and looked at the large tool bench and shelves. His eyes went right to the top of the bench, up on a shelf to the right, about six feet off the ground. There sat a red, plastic coffee can. Travis walked over and plucked the can off the shelf. Placing it on the bench, he pried off the top. Inside was a single plastic bank card for an ATM machine.

Their eyes met; hers were puzzled and his were victorious. He placed the card in his pocket and put the lid back on the can. It was returned to the shelf and as they made their way to the side door they heard a car pull into the drive.

"Run!"

The garage door opener started to moan as the door began to lift. Back into the house they stumbled, shutting the door behind them.

"Out the back!"

They ran to the back door and shut it quietly, alarm showing on their faces.

"What's going on?" Danny asked, sensing the panic.

"Follow me, FAST! She's back!"

The four made their way across the back lot at a sprint, reaching the tree line in a matter of seconds. They continued across the vacant side lot, staying well into the trees. As they reached their car, Travis realized that she had not seen them. They tumbled into the car and Kim drove them further down the road, away from the cabin. They reached the turnaround and she stopped, wondering what to do next.

Travis reached into his pocket, pulled out the plastic card, and smiled as he held it up for all to see.

"4649 is the code to Bruce's debit card. He wanted it. I wonder how much is on it?" The kids took a moment to admire the gold card.

"That's what we were looking for?" Susan exclaimed. "Isn't this stealing?"

As the car made its way past the big blue house they realized that they were all safe from detection.

"It's not stealing. I have a story to tell you and I just can't make this stuff up."

Chapter Fourteen

"Hey, pull into the store here...I want to try this card in the ATM."

Travis pointed to an open spot by some recycling dumpsters.

"Danny, come with me. Girls, we'll be right back. Keep a look out for the blond woman in the Mercedes that was back at the house."

The boys got out of the car, strode to the steps on the side of the store porch, and were inside the country store with an air of confidence. The cash machine was just inside the doorway to the right and Travis inserted the card.

"Here goes...4649." He carefully punched in the code and the machine sprang to life. "It's the code, I can't believe it."

Travis smiled at his best friend and pushed the key for the account balance. $52,150 popped up on the screen and both boys let out a whoop. The old lady behind the counter watched them for a moment as they danced around the machine and then she went back to her cigarette and magazine.

"Fifty-two grand and it's all mine!"

The boys ran out of the store and back to the car, giddy with what they had discovered. After they were seated and the car began to move, Danny asked the question that had played on all of their minds.

"Travis, who are you? Really, who are you? How do you figure that all that money is yours?"

The girls knew something was up, and now Kim began to question Travis as well.

"All of what money? What is going on?"

Travis paused for a moment to collect his thoughts, weighing carefully the option of telling the truth or making something up. He didn't want his friends to view him as a freak and he didn't want to scare them. He was mostly worried about how Kim would react as he didn't want to lose the first girlfriend he ever had.

"Like I said back there, I have a story to tell you and I couldn't make this up if I wanted to."

****

"Ed, can I talk to you a minute?"

The senior financial planner looked up and motioned his partner's former secretary into the office. She closed the door quietly behind her. Fast Eddie was finishing up a phone call and could not be interrupted.

"Tell her to sell everything, to cash out as soon as the authorization comes through."

There was a pause as someone was explaining something on the other end of the line.

"That's fine. I can handle the whole situation myself then. I will go up this weekend and get the signatures. It's no problem...just sell the securities, all of them."

Ed Payne placed the receiver back on its cradle and turned his attention to the secretary.

"What can I do for you, Carol?"

The senior partner gave her the creeps, it always seemed like there was a double entendre to everything he said. Everything always seemed so sexual when he said it.

"Ed, I found something kind of strange. There was a withdrawal from Bruce Nickel's cash account in the amount of two hundred and fifty dollars. I have no idea who could have made it, the card has been dormant since he passed."

"I would guess it was Faith." the planner suggested with confidence as he leaned back and glanced out of the twenty-seventh story window to admire the view of downtown Minneapolis. The secretary pursued the topic further with some hesitation.

"Bruce always told me that no one else had the code for the cash card except me, and I don't know where the card is. I haven't touched a dime of the money in that account…it was his own personal play money." She was scared that the new boss would think she was embezzling from her former boss.

"I know you didn't take any cash. Two hundred and some odd dollars is little to worry about. I'm sure Faith has the card and is living off the cash in the account. I am supposed to get signatures to liquidate his investments, I will be going up to the lake this weekend. Don't worry, I'm sure everything is fine."

He nodded with a smile as an assuring gesture toward the older woman and he brushed her off as quick as he could.

"Please close the door as you go, I have a few more calls to make before I call it a day."

The secretary left with little thought to what had just transpired, it was apparent that whatever had happened in the account was no big deal. At least she would not be suspected of stealing from her former boss.

"I wonder what the hell is going on. Faith wasn't supposed to have that card and I know he didn't give her the security code. He wouldn't give her access to that money in a million years. It's just him and me…I haven't touched a dime. Who in the world has access to the cash? Are they going to report the money? This is not good."

The senior partner's mind was reeling because if someone else in accounting found out about the fun money, things could get dicey. It was never much, a couple hundred here or there moving every month into the private account. No one had to know, it was really nothing more than additional compensation without taxation, something that both men felt they were entitled to after working so hard for so many years.

"It's really nothing more than an under the table bonus for two well deserving partners."

He would get to the bottom of this situation quickly as he was sure that Faith had found the card and must have found the code written somewhere. Even though she wasn't the brightest bulb on the tree, she could always find a way to get more money. Her spending habits were deadly and if she hadn't been such a tremendous trophy for Bruce she would have been gone long ago. He would just have to ask her about the card and then shut the account down.

"Or I can play it another way. Keep stocking the account with spending money for her while I transfer Bruce's assets into my accounts...she won't figure it out until it's too late. He would have wanted me to have the money anyways, he never really trusted her."

A smile played its way across his face as he turned back toward the window, enjoying his status in life. All he had to do was convince her to transfer the securities to him for safe keeping and management with the promise of a money stream for her. It was an easy proposition if he played it right.

****

"You see, I have his thoughts and past in my head and sometimes it comes out as a dream or sudden thought. I can't really control it, it just happens."

The three friends didn't know what to think. They knew Travis had a medical condition, but they never grasped the transplant part of it. The thought of someone else's brain in Travis' head was freaking them out.

"How much of you is you, and how much of you is this old guy, this Bruce?" Kim asked with apprehension, not knowing if she really wanted to know the answer. Travis smiled at her as he responded to all the people in the car.

"I'm Travis, I am me...plain and simple. Part of my brain is still in there, but the old man's brain has allowed me to be normal again, like before I was injured." He went for the solemn sympathy play to put them at ease.

"You guys would probably not want to hang around with me if you knew the old me, the injured me. Kids would make fun of me, they called me a "retard". Now I am normal again...I am very lucky and very thankful."

He said this quietly and the friends became quiet. A tear formed at the corner of Kim's eye and she reached across to hold his hand. The friends in the back sat quietly and processed the situation.

"Everything will be fine." Travis thought to himself.

Chapter Fifteen

Ed Payne pulled his BMW onto the freeway and left the skyscrapers in his rearview mirror. He always drove too fast but seemed to have luck on his side while driving; very rarely was he ever pulled over. He even had the fortune once to be pulled over by a state trooper who was also his client. A warning was sufficient and he went about his speedy way.

It was summertime in Minnesota and he was eager to get to the lake and enjoy some rest and relaxation. He was also eager to get together with Faith. Her body kept running through his mind and he found it hard to concentrate on his driving. A four-hour drive was completed in three and a half and he was all smiles as he turned onto the dirt road and into the driveway of the big, blue house.

There was nobody home.

"What the hell? She knew I was coming up today!"

He was enraged as he looked over the front of the house and made his way across the drive and around the back. He was expecting a big welcome and a whole lot more, suddenly he was all alone and looking at a busy lake.

"If she wants to play this game and use me I will take her for everything…she won't get a damn dime."

The property was silent despite all the activity on the lake. He got back in his Beemer and decided to try the winery down the road; maybe she was waiting there with some nice red wine for them to share. He pulled into the full lot and made his way through the entrance. The barmaid recognized him from many days gone past.

"Hi Ed! How are you doing?"

He smiled, proud that he was recognized in front of many of the patrons that lived around the lake.

"*I am somebody!*" With a swagger in his step he pulled up a seat at the small bar and ordered up a glass of red.

"Say, you haven't happened to see Faith in here today, have you?"

The barmaid paused to reflect and replied with a low, seductive voice, wondering if a night with Ed was a possibility.

"I don't think that girl has been in here all summer. She never comes around since Bruce has been gone. Rumor around town is that she is seeing the sheriff's deputy…I think his name is Troy. Sounds like they have been REALLY friendly. She didn't waste much time getting back on her feet after Bruce died."

This sudden revelation sent a jolt through his brain. *"It all makes sense. She's never around, never available...she's avoiding me. She has found someone else."* A voice snapped him back to reality.

"Hey, are you alright? You tuned out there...can I refill your glass?" He said nothing in response, he just slowly nodded as his reply.

He sipped at his glass and looked around the establishment; he didn't recognize many people. It wasn't his manner to recognize, rather it was his forte to be recognized. He finished his wine and left a tip on the bar, then made his way outside. He drove back to the house and found it empty, then began digging through his briefcase for a photo that was very important to him.

"There he is...the kid."

Ed had worried that the card had fallen into the wrong hands and had also worried that maybe Faith was using it and would deny it. He made a quick call to an old colleague who was working at FirstBank and they ran the card and security number in the system. The camera on the ATM that was used had provided a good picture of the young man who had now taken out almost three thousand dollars from Bruce Nickel's account.

****

Travis Adamson was quickly becoming the most popular kid in the senior class at Twin Lakes High School. He was dressing impeccably and his girlfriend was suddenly the picture of fashion as well. They were the popular couple that everyone else wanted to be. Susan and Danny rounded out the quartet that seemed to rule the school; it was good to be popular.

Summers in this tourist town were an occasion and the kids were blessed to be in the middle of some of the most exciting attractions in Minnesota. They were dreading the beginning of the school year that was quickly approaching; they made the most of every day by hitting the beach or cruising the main drag in town. Small withdrawals were becoming larger as Travis began to indulge himself with more expensive gifts.

A Les Paul guitar was a prize purchase and he was now paying fifty dollars a lesson to learn how to play it. His mother was unsuspecting as she was working as many hours as she could to afford their small but neat house in the middle of town. He began to contemplate purchasing a pick-up truck but he did not have his driver's license yet. That would have to take place after school opened in the fall.

On a bright summer morning at the beginning of August, Emma Harris paid him a visit at his house, rousting him from a lazy sleep. The doctor had been experiencing her busiest summer in years. Between organ harvest and trips to the cities and beyond for surgical procedures, she had temporarily forgotten about her patient up north. After a stressful week in Chicago, she flew back to Minneapolis and then drove up north. She realized that a check-up with Travis was long overdue.

She opened her med bag and did a quick check of his vital stats, but she was much more interested in how he was thinking and feeling.

"Have you had any more dreams or visions from Bruce?"

The key question had been asked and Travis took the time to explain everything that had happened with 4649. He conveniently left out the fact that the account was full of money that he was helping himself to, or the fact that money kept showing up in the account every two weeks.

"So, you are basically telling me that you found a cash card of Bruce's and you are not helping yourself to the money in the account? You have no idea how much is in there? I think you are playing me for a fool young man!" She smiled at him but he knew she was serious.

"Well, maybe I have withdrawn a little...but it is my money after all, right? It's Bruce's and now Bruce is a part of me. Shouldn't I be able to withdraw at least part of it?

The good doctor gave him a stern look and reprimanded him.

"That's not how this works, not even close. That money has to go through probate, it's part of his estate. Someone, an heir or next of kin is entitled to it. If he had a wife, she is entitled to it. It is probably detailed in his will."

Travis smiled, he was now one up on her in regard to the situation.

"It's not detailed in the will. Faith doesn't know a thing about it. I...I mean Bruce...didn't tell her about it. It's his own personal stash."

"How do you know that?" she asked, curious as to what the young man was into.

"Bruce told me all I need to know about the card. I had some more dreams about Ed and me."

She was confused now. "Wait, wait. You talked to Bruce? Who's Ed?" Travis smiled and explained

"Bruce has been in a lot of my dreams lately. Ed is my business partner and best friend. We went to school together at St. John's, then became financial planners, then partners. He's the best."

This information caught Dr. Harris by surprise because the dreams were supposed to be diminishing in frequency and intensity, yet the young patient was indicating the opposite.

"How many dreams have you been having lately?" He looked at her, then looked away.

"Is it a problem if I have had a lot lately?" She looked him in the eyes and paused. He focused on her.

"How many?" Travis knew it wouldn't be good to lie to her, there could be something wrong.

"They come every night."

Chapter Sixteen

Ed booked a room at the Holiday Inn by Twin Lakes, deciding that the last thing he wanted was a confrontation with Faith and her law enforcement boyfriend. He wasn't sure if he believed the barmaid at the winery, but things suddenly made plenty of sense to him. It was time to find the kid that was taking all of Bruce's money.

He felt tired and dirty and so he took a fifteen-minute hot shower and changed into some comfortable clothes. A loose polo shirt, a pair of cargo shorts, and a pair of sandals made him feel like he was on vacation. Ed then took his briefcase full of information and pictures and decided to check out the town. The first stop was a frozen yogurt shop that he recognized as a chain of stores with really good stuff.

The shop was empty except for a young teen who was working the front counter and she greeted him with a smile and a standard company line. *"Perfect, all she has to do is talk and I'll find him."*

Ed returned her smile and in his most comforting voice asked her for a sample of the chocolate caramel frozen yogurt. She gave him a very small cup, about the size of a shot glass and instructed him to help himself. He wandered down the line of self-serve machines and filled his cup with a sample and then moved back to the counter and pulled out a photo of Travis that had been taken earlier by the ATM.

"Say, you seem to be an intelligent young lady. You wouldn't happen to know this kid, would you?" Her face lit up instantly with the recognition of the boy in the picture but she fell suddenly silent.

"Why do you want to know, sir?"

Ed smiled his most comforting smile and relaxed up against the counter.

"He's wanted for armed robbery."

The young girl suddenly sported an alarmed look and he laughed lightly.

"I'm just kidding, of course. He's actually the son of an old friend of mine and I have some money to give him...an inheritance of sorts. It's very important that I find him."

She looked into his eyes and figured that she could trust him; she liked his humor and he seemed harmless.

"That's Travis Adamson...he's a classmate of mine. He's so cool!" She was gushing over the thought of him.

"Any idea where I can find him?"

"Yeah, he lives over on Poplar street, right off the lake about two blocks. A small, white house with an open porch in the front. Do you need me to show you after I get off work?"

He grinned and assured her that he could find the house himself, thanked her for the sample, and bought a large cup for the trouble. It was money well spent.

He sat in his car and slowly ate the frozen deliciousness, savoring every spoonful. It was a guilty vice of his, anything chocolate or any ice cream was an addiction to him. Frozen yogurt was fat free and so he felt no guilt when ordering the large cup of calories. Aside from an addiction to pretty women and a little too much booze, this was the worst thing he had to combat.

The drive to the Adamson house took less than five minutes and he found himself pulled up to the curb in front of the white rambler.

The coolness of an early September night had fallen over the neighborhood and there was an eerie stillness on this block. No one was out, no one was around. He surveyed the house; no movement, no car in the drive.

"Shit, just my luck. Drive all the way up here, book a hotel room, and the kid's not even around."

Ed was antsy now, partly discouraged and partly mad as he got out of his car and walked up to the porch. He ascended the wooden steps and knocked on the white, wooden door. Travis opened it and the older man barged into the opening and raised his voice.

"It's you! You're the kid that's been taking Bruce's money!"

Travis fell back from the door and prepared to defend himself while wearing a broad smile across his face.

"Ed! How the hell are you! It's great to see you!"

The young man moved forward quickly to embrace his visitor but was rebuffed with a shove.

"Where's your parents? Do they know you steal?" The older man's face was a deep red and he was having a hard time concealing his fury.

"Ed! It's me, Bruce! I know you don't…" The intruder cut him off.

"You're not Bruce! What the hell are you talking about? You stole his money!"

Ed slammed the door behind him and prepared to face off with the kid. Travis just smiled, so happy to see his long-lost friend.

"But Ed, you don't understand. Bruce died, but his brain is in here!" The young man pointed to his head and Ed jolted back slightly, puzzled.

"Bullshit. Yeah, Bruce is dead, but you are stealing his money. How did you get the card? The access code?"

"That's what I'm trying to tell you, buddy. The brain keeps telling me stuff. Let me prove it to you."

Travis paused and his brain went into overload as it recognized his old best friend.

"Remember that time, freshman year at St. John's...when we roomed together? Father Zach caught you with Ellen Smith in our room...I had to stay next door with Jerry and Curt so you could...you know?"

Travis was giggling and Ed smiled at the event that had been buried in his mind for so long.

"So, you know one thing about me...hell, with the internet today you could know my whole life as well as I do."

The old man was not about to believe the young thief.

"Bet no one knows this. You got her pregnant and we had to find a solution to get you out of trouble. We took her into St. Cloud to have everything taken care of. Nobody knows that, Ed...it's always been our secret."

Ed became very somber, very sad at the recollection that was still so painful from the distant past.

"But, on a happier note, you and I graduated and over time went into business together. I was your best man in both of your weddings and you were there as my best man when I married Faith. We have been best friends for a long time Ed...a very long time."

The old man felt dejected and confused; he didn't know what to believe, he certainly could have never dreamt of this happening. Travis moved forward slowly and put his arms around his best friend and he felt his brain giving off some great vibes.

"Let's have a drink."

Ed interrupted him with an agitated scowl.

"You're too young to drink...besides, what is my drink of choice? My poison..."

The young man nodded to his friend and confidently smiled.

"That's easy, Ed. A Manhattan on the rocks, bourbon...not rye...preferably Maker's Mark."

The older man chuckled as he recalled how many times they would mix their own at the office and on vacation at the big, blue house.

"So, it's really you? Bruce is in there? He still lives on?"

Travis nodded again with a beaming smile.

Chapter Seventeen

"Rad. I keep seeing this word. Rad." Travis shrugged his shoulders as his friends listened in around the lunch table.

"Don't look at me...I have NO idea!" Kim blurted as she returned his quizzical look. "You know, you have been acting really weird lately, Trav."

He didn't like the rebuttal from his girlfriend while in the company of the whole group. The embarrassed young man had to work hard to control his temper and not verbally snap at Kim. Frustration clouded his mind but he fought to keep his composure.

"I'm sorry, Kimmy... I just can't seem to get it out of my head."

She leaned into his shoulder and whispered in her most seductive voice.

"I can make you forget all about Rad." This brought a smile to his face as he looked at her devilish grin.

"I'll bet you can." he whispered back, trying to keep their dialogue secret while his mind spun into teenage lust.

"Ok, you two…enough of that!" Susan had overheard the whole thing and was a little jealous of their relationship. She gave a glance to Danny next to her and he was oblivious of the whole exchange, seemingly deep in thoughts of his own.

"Hey, dreamer…what gives?" Travis tried to snap his friend back into the present.

"I was just thinking, you know? Rad…could be short for radical. Maybe your new brain from this Bruce guy proves he was a hippy or something…a radical, you know?"

Travis looked down at the remainder of his mystery lunch and shook his head.

"I don't think so, Dan. I think it stands for something…I get the weird feeling that it is short for something important."

Most of the lunch table got up at the same time and carried their partially empty trays back to the dish line. After ditching their mess it was on to fifth hour and more school; Travis and Dan had Chemistry class and they settled into a monotone lecture from a teacher that had mentally retired five years earlier.

"I'm going to ask Dr. Emma about Rad, she might know something."

As he finished whispering to his buddy in front of him the teacher paused and called him out.

"Is there a problem, Mr. Adamson?"

Everybody's eyes turned to the senior student, who was quickly assessing the equation on the board. Bruce's brain kicked in and bailed the youngster out.

"Yes, I am confused as to the balance in your equation. You show what appears to be an ionic bond, yet I thought it was supposed to be covalent. I must be confused."

Travis had no idea where the words came from, it seemed from somewhere deep within him. The veteran teacher bought the diversion and proceeded to drone on with a five-minute answer to Travis' question, much to the dismay of the rest of the class. The bell rang and bailed everybody out of the boring lecture.

"Hey Trav. Did you see Rhonda Peterson checking you out? She's got a thing for you...I think she even threw you a wink." Travis blushed, he was caught by his friend in the middle of the interesting interlude.

"Knock it off, Dan...it's no big thing." His friend realized that he had hit a nerve and was going to give him a good-natured ribbing.

"No big thing? Tell that to Kimmy. You were flirting back, weren't you?" All Travis could do was smile, he was caught by his best friend.

"Not a word, you hear? Not a word."

The hallway was absolute chaos as the students were all gathering up their backpacks and heading for the busses and parking lot. Then she appeared and the boys all froze to check her out; this was now a daily routine. Travis and Dan stopped what they were doing and they saw her approaching; the beautiful, young brunette teacher with the knockout figure.

"Mmm, Ms. Weston." Travis murmured this aloud to his friend and then looked to find Kim. She was not in sight. He turned to his best friend and gave him a sly smile.

"Watch this."

Danny looked at his friend and realized that Bruce was back.

"No...Trav, no..." but it was too late.

Travis moved into the center of the hallway, a few steps in front of the rookie teacher. Everything stopped. She looked at him and smiled out of courtesy as she had no clue of what would happen next. Travis moved forward slowly, two steps brought him face to face with her, and he planted the most passionate kiss he could muster on her soft lips.

She stood frozen, shocked by what had happened, and her hand came up to land a solid slap on the side of his face. It echoed in the suddenly quiet corridor and the cheers erupted from the spectators.

The young woman was paralyzed in fear for a moment and then ducked into the closest classroom, confused and embarrassed. Travis and Dan headed out the nearest door to the parking lot as congratulatory howls and pats on the back were given by a majority of the spectators. They stopped at the pickup truck.

"What the hell, Trav? What did you do that for? Did you see the look on her face? Seriously, that was messed up, dude!" Travis turned to his friend and studied his disappointed expression for a moment. Then Bruce came out.

"Yeah, you're right, Dan...that wasn't very nice. You know what, though? You only live once...you have to take what you want. You only get one chance and before you know it, boom! It's gone. I wanted that. She'll get over it, just wait and see. I just got what every kid...including you...wanted back there. I just made it happen. No guts, no glory."

****

Travis made it to his appointment at the clinic with two minutes to spare and, much to his relief, Dr. Emma was stuck in a procedure with Seth, her assistant. She met him in the lobby five minutes later, still wearing light blue scrubs that had seen a little too much use. Both of them walked to the back and sat down in her office, the break was welcome for both.

131

"Can I get you anything, Trav?" Dr. Harris was being a gracious host and was happy that her star client was making better progress than anyone could have imagined.

"A Mountain Dew would be great." the young man requested politely, hoping a caffeine dose would get him moving. She returned with two cans of soda and began her series of questions.

"How are the headaches? Last time we talked they were starting to bother you...any change?"

The headaches were becoming more intense but were not increasing in frequency and the young patient did not want to alarm his doctor. The last thing he wanted was a "headache" with her in the form of a lecture.

"They're not a big deal...I get one every once and a while, usually after exercise...but it's no big deal." The doctor's face wore a skeptical expression.

"Let me be the judge of that. How often do they occur?"

"Gee Doc, it's only about once a week, and only when I exercise...not a big deal." She shifted in her chair and studied him, looking for something that would indicate a lie.

"Any blurred vision?"

Travis took a long drink from his can and smiled.

"No blurred vision. Hey, I don't mean to change the subject, but…"

The doctor let out a small laugh.

"Yeah, sure you don't!"

The patient smiled and continued.

"I have been having this reoccurring thought, almost a dreamlike chant running through my head. I can't seem to get rid of it. Rad…Rad. I keep thinking of the word Rad."

"Hmm. Rad, huh? Short for radical. Maybe you're a closet radical…a political dissident? Have you had the urge to protest?" She was messing with him now and he was glad that she had moved on from the headache talk.

"Nope. It's not radical, I know that. It's something else." Dr. Harris gave it a moment and then summoned her assistant, Seth.

The tall, lanky, doctor in his early thirties appeared in the office doorway with a helpful smile.

"What's up, guys?" Emma figured he might be of help and she was right.

"Travis keeps thinking of the word RAD…any idea what that could mean? He says it's not short for Radical."

Seth gave a tired shrug, rubbed his temples with the palms of his hands, and replied with solid reasoning.

"Why not Google it? Run the word on the Net."

Travis and the doctor looked at each other with foolish expressions, wondering why they hadn't thought of that. Seth pulled his cellphone from his pant pocket and typed in the information.

"Says here its short for radical. Wait, it's also an abbreviation of sorts...it stands for Remote Assistance Device. Hmm." The patient and his doctor listened intently and then waited for Seth to continue.

"Remote Assistance Device...yeah, RAD. It's the thing that works with computerized machines to direct them."

He looked at the two sitting in their cozy chairs and saw two blank looks being returned.

"Remote, you know?!"

They both shook their heads slowly, not understanding where he was going.

"Say you have something motorized, like a remote car. The RAD allows you to control it by remote. Those little vacuums that run on their own all over the house...that's RAD. The little R2D2 things at the golf course that cut the grass without anyone driving them...that's RAD. I saw a rich dude at a lake party once playing with one of these. Pretty cool stuff."

The assistant smiled proudly, knowing he had bested them in the information department.

"Alright. Thanks Einstein!" Dr. Emma was giving her assistant a little admiration and grief at the same time and he liked it. He disappeared down the hallway, whistling the whole way.

"Why in the world would I be thinking about a RAD? Remote control? Weird." Travis was thinking out loud and Emma was too tired to continue with this train of conversation.

"Travis, have the headaches become worse, more intense?"

He was barely listening to her as he shook her off, wanting to get out of the office and pursue this new idea further.

"No, Doc, I'm ok, really."

She realized that she was making little progress and so she let him go. He found his way to the parking lot and was on his way to Danny's house in a hurry.

"Dan, Dan!" he called out to his best friend as he approached him from around the side of the house. His friend was cleaning up the back yard with his younger brother and neither boy looked like they were enjoying the task.

"What's up, Brainiac?" he responded, dropping the lawn rake in a seeming fit of disgust.

"You're not going to believe this." The tired teen put both hands on his hips and replied slowly.

"Try me."

Chapter Eighteen

"Ed. It's Travis...I mean Bruce...you know? I'm going to be down in the Cities on Friday for a checkup and some tests. Can we talk? I had another dream and I'm scared. We really have to talk."

Ed had taken a liking to the kid and since no more money was going out of the account, he seemed to trust him. He was still skeptical about whether Travis was Bruce or not, but he started to think about the kid like his own.

"Sure Travis, call me when you get to town and we can meet up. Don't worry, we will take care of whatever the problem is...ok?"

Travis hung up and felt some relief. The dreams were more vivid and were coming back every night. He wasn't sleeping well and his temper was growing difficult. His relationship with Kim was hitting some turbulence and the word around school was that Rhonda Peterson was making moves on him. Most people could agree that Rhonda Peterson was the hottest girl in the junior class, if not the whole school. Travis' sudden popularity was going to his head.

Friday arrived and, after a battery of tests and prodding from various doctors, Travis was finally free to spend the afternoon with Dr. Emma. Dinner time led them to one of the nicest steakhouses in Minneapolis and Ed was waiting at a private booth when they arrived. After exchanging pleasantries and an introduction between the older business man and the famous doctor, food was ordered and they got down to serious discussion.

"Hey Ed, guess what?"

The graying man smiled, genuinely interested in what the young man was up to. Travis continued, much to the dismay of his doctor. Emma Harris shot him a sideways glance, knowing what was coming next.

"I'm on the football team! I'm the kicker! It's the only thing they will let me do... they're worried about me getting hit or hitting someone."

Ed smiled, thinking back to the days at St. John's where both him and Bruce played. Bruce was much better than him, as he barely left the bench for the field. Bruce had been a Division Three All-American."

"Geez, kid...that's great! Aren't you a little scared about getting hit though?" It was clear that Doctor Harris was not happy with this latest arrangement.

"Nobody, and I mean NOBODY ever hits the kicker...kinda boring but I have kicked six extra points and two field goals, one from twenty-seven yards!" It was also very obvious that football had become Travis' new passion and it added to his popularity.

"You know, Bruce was a hell of a player at SJU. He was one of the best linebackers they ever had." Travis smiled as his 'Bruce' brain opened back up.

"Hey, remember that time we were at Gustavus and we were tied in the fourth quarter...21 all if I remember right...and I picked off the screen pass and took it all the way? God that was great! Totally changed the game, we won big and got a share of the conference title."

Ed nodded; he remembered it from the bench.

"You were All-American that year."

Bruce wanted to give his best friend some credit also.

"You were a good player too, Ed. You just never got the chance you deserved." Ed smiled at the graciousness of the statement and turned to Emma Harris.

"I wasn't very good...I was much better in the dorm rooms at St. Ben's than I was on the field." Both men chuckled and Ed had a gleam in his eyes as he sized up the attractive female doctor. Bruce clarified the statement with a smile.

"St. Ben's is the women's college across the road from SJU...Ed spent many an evening there." The doctor nodded and smiled at the two men reliving old glories from days gone past. Then Travis returned.

"Say Ed...I had some more dreams this week. One keeps coming back. It's the crash...I can't ever get control of my car. It's so weird, so vivid...I can't seem to fall back asleep. Something was wrong...I shouldn't have died."

Ed was suddenly very somber and quiet, his eyes started to water up.

"I can't imagine what you went through...I wish I was there to help you somehow."

Dr. Harris took this moment to lend clarity to the situation.

"There was nothing you could have done. Bruce passed away on impact...we were on the scene quickly and took the proper measures to save his organs. You are the benefactor, Travis."

The young man was not smiling, he looked like he was about to break into tears as well. Things got very quiet for a moment and then Travis spoke up.

"Ed, what do you know about RAD?" Ed's focus changed with the question from the young man. An expression of surprise overcame the older man.

"RAD is an incredible development that you...I mean Bruce, and I had invested in. Bruce used to drive his boat, his lawnmower, all kinds of stuff with the RAD."

Travis and Dr. Harris exchanged interested glances and let Ed continue.

"He…Bruce…was obsessed with the thing. He had the prototype for the next generation in RAD, he called it RAD 2, and he was messing with it all the time up at the lake. It was his pet project, his baby when he wasn't setting up investment deals. He was ready to take it to market with a firm in Chicago, they wanted to buy it from him and he wanted twenty million up front with a percentage of sales…I think something like two and a half percent on every sale."

Ed continued describing the situation to an intrigued audience of two.

"The whole thing fell apart after he passed…it just disappeared. I asked Faith about it and she had no idea. I checked his office and his home and never found it. It just disappeared." The older man shook his head, still not comprehending what could have happened to it over a year later.

"How did the thing work?" Travis asked quietly, with an overwhelming desire to know more.

"It was pretty simple, yet complex. Kind of a weird thing. All you needed to do was hook up the RAD to anything with a computer and the RAD would integrate its controls into the system. It was a small, black box with wires and clamps…Bruce would wire it into a computer on a device and he could control it with a joystick looking thing. It was like his ultimate video game or radio-controlled toy. He'd drive his speedboat all over the lake with no one at the wheel…people on the lake would lose their minds!"

The food was served and savored with everyone enjoying their company and stories. The time passed quickly and Ed had to leave for a business engagement, although Travis suspected it was to meet a woman. The old man made sure to get Emma Harris' number on a card for future reference; she suspected that he wanted to meet up with her at a later date. The man was a player.

Travis and Dr. Emma returned to their hotel rooms after sundown and he regretted missing the football game back home due to his medical situation. It wasn't a problem; he called Danny to get the update after ten o'clock and found out that Twin Lakes had won by forty points.

He placed his next call to Kim and spent over an hour on the phone talking about all the things that teenagers talk about. They were missing each other and promised to get together as soon as he returned to town. It was well after midnight when Travis fell asleep with thoughts of his girl running through his mind.

****

The dream came on quickly. Bruce and Ed were standing on the dock behind the big, blue lake home. Bruce had the controls and the speedboat was doing large circles in the middle of the lake. Ed had a drink in his hand and was standing in a wobbly manner at the end of the dock, laughing in intoxication.

"Hey Ed, what do you think of RAD 2? We should really do something crazy…we should hook this frickin' thing up to my car!" Both men were laughing, lost in the haze of too many drinks.

Faith was laying next to them on the parked pontoon with a bikini that was showing off way too much skin. The men were enjoying every move she made and Bruce was anticipating getting her alone later that evening. As for now, they were playing with the toy and coming up with their next big caper. She listened intently, flirting with both men as she adjusted her top to give them a better view of her purchased assets. She knew exactly what she was doing and smiled with the pride of a thousand-dollar hooker.

****

"Doc! Doc! Wake up! We gotta talk!"

The door that adjoined both rooms was locked and it took a moment for Emma Harris to come to and recognize where she was. She rolled over and checked the time on the bed side alarm clock; it was 2:24 in the morning. *"What in the hell is going on?!"* Emma was not happy, in fact she was pissed off.

"What do you want!" she screamed in a weird whispery way to not wake anyone else. She unlatched the door and opened it slightly.

"Doc! I just had another dream...fuckin' A." She recoiled with his language.

"Travis, watch your language." He looked extremely confused and uncomfortable as he was pacing on his side of the doorway.

"God. It was so VIVID! Ed and I...I mean Bruce. We were going to hook up the RAD to my...I mean Bruce's...car. Did I...I mean Bruce...screw up and kill himself with the RAD?!" He looked like he was about to vomit.

"Travis, sit down on the bed. Let me get you a glass of water...just relax. Breathe."

Travis called Ed as the sun was rising on a beautiful Saturday morning in Minneapolis. Ed was not happy to be rousted, he had planned on another hour or two of sleep followed by some extra-curriculars with the brunette next to him, and then maybe a good breakfast or lunch depending on how things progressed. He picked up the receiver and recognized the young man right away.

"Is everything ok?" he asked, hoping for no problems.

"Yeah, Ed...I think so. I'm sorry to bother you but I have to ask you something. Did you and Bruce ever hook the RAD up to a car?"

It took a moment or two for the question to register in his foggy brain, then Ed tried to recollect all the things they did.

"Yeah, we hooked it up to his car once or twice and drove it around the church parking lot at the end of the road, up by the lake home." He paused and got out of bed gently, hoping to not waken his guest. He walked lightly to the bathroom and then continued his train of conversation.

"It was really cool, actually. You know how cars drive themselves today, in certain situations? We were playing with the RAD2 and were thinking of how to run a whole series of transportation vehicles the way air traffic controllers direct airplanes in airspace. We thought we were on to something before Bruce passed." There was an uncomfortable silence at the end of the line.

"Ed. Do you think Bruce was playing with the RAD2 and had an accident? Do you think he might have killed himself?" Another long silence followed on the line.

"Nope. I doubt it. He had lost the RAD2 a week earlier...he couldn't seem to find it and he was in a panic. He was supposed to do a demonstration in Chicago at the beginning of February and he was working out some kinks. He didn't know where it was and he was really pissed at himself. We searched the lake home, his home in the Cities, and even our office complex. Somebody probably took it not even knowing what it was."

"Ed. Are you sure he didn't accidently kill himself?" Another long pause.

"Travis, there is no way he killed himself...he had an accident. Think about it. Why would he be in the car with the remote-control unit? He would be driving it from outside the vehicle...he would be using the RAD2 from a location near where the car would be driving. It was at night...he would not test the car on a roadway at night. No way...he did not kill himself accidentally, or on purpose, if that's what you're thinking.

Chapter Nineteen

His arrival was a surprise to her as he pulled into the circular driveway. She was not expecting him and now was reeling with fear. *"What in God's name is HE doing here? What does HE want?"*

She did her best to compose herself before he reached for the doorbell and, after a second ring, she appeared in the entry way and took his breath away. She was still as stunning as she was the last time he had seen her. He wanted her the moment she appeared through the glass doorframe.

"Ed, my gosh, what a pleasant surprise! What brings you here?" She put on her best smile and brought forth a charm that would take over his willpower.

"Faith, it's so nice to see you. You look absolutely breathtaking! Beautiful! It's been a long time!"

She opened the screen door and let him into the foyer. He took a moment to check her out from head to toe and then moved in for an embrace. She placed her arms around him awkwardly, not wanting to get too close to him and lead him on. She would have preferred that he never show up; now she felt stuck with him.

"So, again…what do I owe this visit to?" Ed knew at that moment he probably had no chance with her; the rumors were true.

"I was just in the area and thought I'd stop by." He tried a little charm with her and she recoiled slightly, repulsed.

"No, seriously though. I thought I'd stop and check to see how you have been and to get a couple of things that we need at the firm. Bruce had some stuff that we would like back."

He gauged her expression and body language, wondering how she would react to this request.

"What kind of things do you need, Ed?" He paused for effect and then threw the big request out.

"I am looking for the RAD2. Remember the device that Bruce and I were working on, the remote-control tool. A small, black box…about this size?"

He held his hands out and tried to provide a visual for her. He knew that she knew what he was talking about, she had seen it many times and had been privy to their conversations and plans.

"Gee, Ed…I haven't seen that thing since before Bruce passed away. I have no idea where it could be…it's not around here." Her expression turned to sorrow and Ed saw through the charade instantly.

"Haven't seen it, huh? That's too bad...really too bad. We just had an offer of twenty million for the thing and you would stand to inherit Bruce's portion. Ten mill...not a bad deal for either of us, huh? Gosh, that's too bad." He looked her in the eyes and paused for effect again.

"Will you do me a big favor and give me a call if it turns up again?"

She nodded and made sure to embrace him more enthusiastically while hoping he would get out of her house. Her mind was flying aimlessly over the prospect of ten million dollars for the stupid little toy that they used to play with on the lake. Ed played the situation to the best of his ability and left promptly. He would have to sit down with Travis and the beautiful Dr. Harris to plan out their next move.

****

First hour Senior Creative Writing was the last place that Travis Adamson wanted to be on a Monday morning in October. The events of the weekend were still playing in his head and he knew that something fishy was going on. His phone call with Ed from two days earlier was still running through his mind.

"I didn't kill myself and it wasn't an accident...what in the world happened?"

He appeared to be deep in literary thought and so his teacher, Mrs. Melville, didn't want to bother him. He kept

149

running every possibility through his mind. Now he was hoping for a dream every night, a dream that would solve the whole mystery.

"Bruce is trying to tell me something…there's more to this story. What is Bruce trying to tell me?"

Second hour was study hall with Kim and Danny; Travis couldn't wait to tell them everything from the weekend. Deep in the recesses of his mind, Bruce's mind, he knew he had to revisit the blue house by the lake. There was more to find and it seemed like his mind was instructing him to go back to the house.

He flew into Mr. Lemon's study hall room and caught the attention of everyone who had already arrived. The bell rang and the trio of friends retreated to an isolated corner and began to confer.

"Geez, I couldn't wait to get back…I had to stay for a concussion test on Sunday…it totally sucked."

Kim showed her concern immediately.

"Is everything alright?"

Travis nodded and she gave him a tender hug. Danny waited the embrace out and then began to pry into the more interesting details.

"So…what happened? You seem really fired up this morning. What did we miss?"

Travis turned his attention to his best friend.

"Let me tell you, you guys missed a hell of a lot...I met with Ed and got some interesting information. Also, I had another dream and it was really strange."

He spent the next twenty minutes running through all of the details and then they began to plot and plan.

"You really think we need to go back out to the house, huh?" Travis nodded at Kim and she looked less than enthused.

"We almost got caught last time! I don't think I want to do that again!"

Travis looked into her eyes and saw the fear, the apprehension. He then looked to Danny and saw excitement.

"Kim, you don't have to go with. Dan and I will go out there. It's no big deal...we will just take a quick look for the RAD2 and then be out of there before anyone knows it. You do not have to go with, ok?"

The office runner, a senior classmate looking for an easy high school credit, suddenly appeared in the doorway with a pass for Travis. Mr. Lemon took the paper from the girl and delivered it to Travis at the back of the room.

"You can go right now. Principal Nelson is looking for you...I can guess what THIS is about."

The teacher wanted to sound stern, but Travis saw a small smile work across his face. *"Everybody knows."*

He walked into the office, sat at the only open chair in the sterile environment, and within a minute the principal's office door opened.

"Come on in, Travis, we have some things to talk about."

The young student entered this intimidating realm and saw Sylvia, Dr. Emma, and Miss Weston seated at the small conference table on the far side, near the large windows that overlooked the front entryway. He stopped in a panic, fear flooding his brain. The principal gestured to the open seat in the middle, between Sylvia and the doctor. He sat down with a sheepish expression and glanced quickly at Ms. Weston. *"This is not going to be fun."*

****

The boys rumbled north out of town in Danny's rusty old pickup truck; they didn't have to worry about a speeding ticket as the old heap wouldn't go much more than sixty miles an hour on a good day.

"A one-week suspension...they said I was lucky that I wasn't expelled." Dan turned to his friend and smiled.

"Good news then, huh?" He looked back to the road as Travis finished detailing the events of an hour earlier.

"God, Dan...you know that wasn't me that kissed her, right?" Dan chuckled and turned to his friend.

"Sure as hell looked like you, buddy." He nodded for emphasis.

"Yeah, it was me, but it wasn't...that was totally Bruce. I would never do that." The boys suddenly broke down laughing at the idea of what had happened.

The old truck lumbered into Richwood and passed the general store, then hooked a right and headed up toward the church and the lake. It was a lazy, sunny day and no one was really out and about; things looked and felt deserted. All the better for what they had in mind. Danny noticed the anxiety on his friend's face as they approached the curve where Bruce had died.

"Dan, stop here a second...pull over in the church lot."

The young friend did as he was told and Travis surveyed the scene around him carefully. He closed his eyes and breathed in the fresh air from outside his truck window. It seemed like an eternity to Danny before his friend opened his eyes again.

"There is something about this place, Dan. I don't know what it is, but there is something about this place. I keep seeing the church, the playground, and the lot in my dreams...every night."

Danny shifted in the driver's seat uncomfortably. "Can we go now? You're kind of freaking me out a little here."

Travis laughed softly and nodded. "Let's go to the house."

They left the parking lot and headed south to the lake. After a couple of hundred feet they turned east along the lake and were at the circular driveway in a matter of a minute. The boys drove by slowly and surveyed the scene. It was late afternoon and it didn't look like anyone was home.

"Let's go back over to the lot next door where we parked last time. I think that worked pretty good."

Dan drove about a hundred feet further and pulled into the narrow drive that helped him disappear in the trees.

"This is good. Are you ready to do this?" Danny didn't have second thoughts; this was the kind of adventure that made life exciting. They weren't going to steal anything that wasn't theirs, they were just on a mission of discovery so to speak.

The boys made their way through the wooded lot to the edge of the estate. The blue house loomed in front of the both of them and it cast off an eerie calmness.

"Remember, it's a small plastic looking black box, about this big." Travis demonstrated the size with his hands and

Danny nodded. "Let's start at the back door again and head for the garage. I have a feeling that it would be kept there."

They made their way out into the open space while watching the road and drive to their right. After climbing a short set of white stairs to the deck, Travis fished out the spare key from below the planter and let himself into the back of the house.

"Faith?" he called out quietly, not wanting to arouse any neighbors who might have their windows open. There was no answer.

"Ok, let's take a look at the garage." The boys moved up a half a level and quickly crossed the kitchen to the service door and the parking area.

Travis lead the way and when he opened the service door his nostrils were filled with the smell of stale gasoline and old exhaust; it was a welcome smell that brought back memories from Bruce's past.

"It's always kept right over here, in this storage closet by the bench. Follow me."

The boys moved across the garage and opened the tall, steel cabinet with care. The shelf where the RAD2 should have been was empty.

"That's where I always put it." Travis declared as he flashed back to Bruce.

"Shit. Now what? Do we search the whole house?" Dan asked with a bit of exasperation.

"No. It wouldn't be in the house. I wouldn't have left it down by the boat and I don't think Faith would have moved it. IT SHOULD BE RIGHT HERE."

Travis was frustrated as well for it looked like worthless trip. They never heard the car pull up outside of the double garage door until it was too late.

The mechanical lift purred into motion and the door rose before they could react. Both boys froze for an instant as their brains tried to register what was happening. Travis and Dan both pivoted toward the opening and locked eyes with Faith. Her expression told the whole story as she laid on her automobile horn and reached for her phone. The boys could not run by her and out of the front of the garage and so they sprinted back into the house.

She quickly pulled a small handgun from her purse and jumped out of her vehicle.

"Get out of my fucking house!" she screamed as she entered the dwelling, hell bent on shooting the intruders. They ran out the back door and down the steps, taking them two or three at a time. They were almost to the wooded tree line when the first shot rang out. Travis could hear the bullet whiz over his head and hit a tree squarely.

"Holy shit, she's got a gun!"

They disappeared into the wooded lot and she stood on the deck, wondering if she should go after them. After calling the sheriff's office, she retreated into the house to survey the possible damage and theft. The boys knew they couldn't go back across the front of the house; she would identify the pickup truck and they'd be in big trouble.

Dan slowly moved the truck to the roadway and drove further down the lakeshore drive, looking for a place to park and hide. About eight houses down there was one that looked like nobody had been there in a while. The garbage cans had been tipped down into the ditch and the grass was long. Leaves filled the yard and the place looked closed for the winter.

They pulled into the tree lined drive and parked in the yard, behind the garage and away from the road. No one would see them there. They locked the truck and looked around; there was no one home. Travis had been close to here before and now Bruce's brain was directing him again.

"Let's move across the road…right over there. I think we can work our way back to the church and then call Kimmy for a ride."

Travis and Dan moved quickly, making sure to work their way further and further from the blue house.

"Over there, that path will take us to the back of the church." It was all flashing back to Travis; Bruce knew the area well.

The boys moved up to the back of the church and watched as two Becker County squads flew past, careening down the dirt road with their lights on. With a look that combined the thrill of the moment and the terror of getting caught, they crossed over the road carefully and then moved under the cover of the trees and terrain back toward the general store.

Travis called Kim and explained the situation as they kept moving. Another squad went by and Travis recognized the deputy as the guy who visited Faith when he had seen her for the first time.

Travis and Dan passed the store and continued up a short street, passing some small, dilapidated houses along the way. They stopped and waited for Kim; she showed up twenty minutes later with her small car. The tension was broken when the boys got into the vehicle.

"Let's hurry up and get out of here. The crazy bitch almost shot us!" Kim wore an expression of alarm but the boys were laughing hysterically.

Chapter Twenty

"Sheriff's office, Deputy Haley speaking."

The young man was handling the incoming calls on the private line as well as covering 911 for the usual dispatcher who had ducked out for a bathroom break and a bite to eat across the street. He had to pull a half hour of duty on the desk and didn't mind the down time. It only hurt if something big broke out because he would be stuck in the office instead of being able to respond. There weren't many big things happening on this evening in Becker County.

"Yeah, Haley. We have to talk." The call was on the private line and Troy Haley was curious as to what would be so pressing, so urgent. The voice on the other end of the line continued.

"I know you did it. I know what happened to Bruce Nickel that night and I know you did it."

The deputy's mind was suddenly reeling and dizziness overcame him.

"What in the hell are you talking about? Who is this?" He tried to control himself, to keep his composure, but he was quickly losing it.

"I know you killed him. I know you are sleeping with his wife. I know the whole thing and the question is simple. What is it worth to you to be able to walk away?"

Haley froze, wondering who could possibly be on the other end of the line.

"This is a joke, right? Real funny, asshole. Prank calls like this to law enforcement can get you in a lot of trouble, buddy!"

The voice on the other end of the line continued, unfazed.

"Listen here, pal. You are in one hell of a lot of trouble...I know it all and I can prove it. But there is one way out. You're going to meet with me, no funny business, and we're going to make a deal. You will win and I will win...we will both win, quite a deal actually. Here's what we are going to do..."

****

Friday nights in Minnesota mean high school football and Travis was excited as he finished his warmups before the game. The opposing team, a conference rival, was warming up on the other end of the field and they were chanting loudly as they tried to intimidate the Lakers.

Being the kicker for the Lakers was a big deal for Travis because it increased his visibility and popularity among his peers. His closest friends were also enjoying being a part of the experience; they all sat together in the student section and made as much noise as they could.

Clad in white and maroon, the opponents won the coin toss at the center of the field and they elected to kick off first. The red and white home team would receive the kickoff and march sixty-five yards down the field for the first score. Now it was Travis' turn to shine as he would have the opportunity to add to the lead by kicking the extra point. The snap from center was true and the placement of the ball on the ground was good and so Travis stepped forward and kicked the football squarely through the uprights. 7-0, the Lakers in the lead.

He didn't have to leave the field though, as he now had to kick the ball downfield to the opposing team. With a line of teammates ready to charge, he ran forward and drove the ball with his foot over forty yards; a nice kick for a high schooler. He stayed back and watched the kick receiver catch the ball and then run for the edge of the field. The kid was little and fast, he made the sidelines before the coverage could get to him. He was flying up the side of the field and the Lakers were out of position, it looked like he might go all the way.

Travis had been told to stay away from the receiver, basically to kick the ball and stand back and watch. This was what he was doing when the quick little kid cut back and ran toward the middle of the field.

"Damn, he's coming at me! Time to light him up!"

The runner was almost nose to nose with Travis when the kicker lunged with all his might. The bodies collided in a crash and the ball popped up into the air. A red and white clad defender fell on the ball and the crowd went wild.

Then everything went silent. The opposing kid got up groggily and stumbled toward his sidelines, not sure where he was. The kicker lay face down at the forty-two yard line and was not moving. Emma Harris froze at the end of the bleachers, her eyes stuck on her patient.

"Oh my god, he's not moving!" she screamed aloud as she ran to the small gate that led to the field.

Then he moved, slow at first. His teammates crowded around him in a hurry and helped him to his feet. The grin on his face was priceless and his buddies started screaming and slapping him on the pads. He stumbled, trying to get a realization of where he was, and then he figured the scenario out. Coaches and teammates were yelling encouragement from the sidelines and the crowd erupted in cheers.

"Hell of a hit, huh guys!" was all he could say, but his expression told the story.

Doc Betters, the athletic trainer, met him halfway to the sidelines and began assessing him before Doctor Harris could get on the field.

"Travis, are you ok? Are you alright?" The young man nodded.

"I feel great, coach! Greatest feeling ever!" Betters expression took on a concerned look.

"Trav, I'm not your coach, I'm Doctor Betters...you know? The trainer? Are you OK?"

The smile never left his face but he was stumbling and trying to keep his balance as he moved off the field.

"Son, you'd better sit down over here."

Chapter Twenty One

"Look, I've got a great deal for you...you would be wise to accept it. All I need is the RAD2. I have a buyer in Chicago that will pay up to twenty million for it and you can have half. I will take Bruce's share that is supposed to go to Faith and you can take the other half...we're talking about ten million apiece before taxes. No one has to know anything except that we made one hell of a business deal. What do you say?"

There wasn't much to say; he just stood there and looked the man over carefully while contemplating what would come next. Silence.

"Look, young man...you called me. You figured this whole thing out...I don't know how, but you did it. Take the deal."

The man shook his head slowly, side to side. "I get the twenty and you go free."

There would be no deal. The older man pulled the loaded .45 from his shoulder holster and fired twice into the man's chest. One bullet was all it took, but he wanted to make sure. The cleanup would be easy because there was no one around. A deserted field away from the lake offered plenty of space to bury the man. He didn't need ten million dollars, he needed anonymity; no one could know what he did.

****

The Monday morning in late October arrived with the brightness of the autumn sun and the newest celebrity at the high school. Travis and Dan pulled into the student parking lot and right away the high fives and hollered acknowledgements started. The big play on Friday night brought him a celebrity status that few high schoolers ever achieve; Travis Adamson was the big man on campus.

He met Kim in the main entry way to the school with a covert kiss, mindful that school staff might be around and he didn't want the hassle of a Public Display of Affection, or PDA. The last thing he needed was an hour of detention and he was sure that the teachers must have gotten bonuses in their paychecks for every PDA they wrote up. The popular couple walked hand in hand down the hallway to first hour.

Halfway through Creative Writing, Mrs. Melville stopped at his desk with a concerned look on her face.

"Travis, are you ok? You don't look so good."

The student had been staring straight ahead with no expression and the color seemed drained from his face.

"Travis, can you hear me?" The lack of a response had the teacher worried and she bent down closer to his face. He suddenly snapped out of his daydream and his hands moved over his eyes.

"Sorry, Mrs. Melville...I don't feel so good. I've got a whale of a headache."

"You need not apologize to me, dear...go down to the nurse and lay down for a while."

She was a nurturing kind of teacher and Travis appreciated her sympathy toward him. He arose slowly from his seat, grabbed his notebook and pen, and moved out into the hallway.

"Are you ok on your own, or should I send someone with you?" the teacher inquired with genuine concern.

"I'm ok, Ma'am...I can get there alright...thank you."

He missed study hall and his friends were concerned. By the middle of third hour he was on his way home after his mom came from work to pick him up. After pulling the shades in his bedroom to keep the intrusive sun out, he snuggled down on his bed into a deep slumber as the pain in his head drifted away. The phone on his nightstand was vibrating with calls from Kim and Danny, but he had turned the ringer off and was unaware of anyone trying to reach him.

His brain took him to a warm summer evening and a party along the lake. The blue house loomed behind him and his friends and he occasionally looked toward it hoping to find his beautiful wife. The RAD2 was on the dock, ready to be hooked up to his pontoon boat. Ed was laughing and drinking his usual too much while pursuing a young lady from the neighboring lake home. A young man was talking to him about his retirement account and an opportunity to invest some money in a get rich quick scheme.

"I'll tell you what, son, this little beauty right here is not a get rich quick scheme. This is the real deal in terms of technology and motion. I can make anything with a computer system do what I want it to, to go where I want it to, at a speed I want it to. This little machine is incredible." Bruce nodded and smiled for effect before continuing his sales pitch.

"What do you do for a living?"

The young man on the dock identified himself as Seth and began talking about his career in the medical field.

"You work right here in town, in the hospital, huh? Good for you! Medicine is a great field to be in right now...this little invention may even revolutionize your field." He nodded again and kept pressing the topic to his new potential investor.

"Ed. Ed! Come over here a minute and meet Seth...he works in Medicine."

The loyal business partner reluctantly moved away from the tanned beauty he was socializing with and sauntered onto the wooden dock structure.

"Medicine, huh? Good for you. Maybe you can cure the massive hangover that I'm going to have in the morning...ha, ha, ha!"

Fast Eddie was wobbly from a few too many drinks and both Bruce and Seth moved to steady him on the walkway over the water. They didn't need a drowning victim on this wonderful evening.

"Ed, I was just telling Seth here about the RAD...the RAD2. What do you think about it?" The inebriated man began spewing the wonderfulness of the new product.

"The best part, young man, is that we already have an offer on it. Illinois Technical Corporation has made a tentative offer of twenty million for this little baby. All we have to do is work the kinks out of it and we will be rich!"

He slurred his words but the young man knew exactly what he said. Bruce tried to seal the deal.

"Seth, this is a great deal. We'll get you in on the ground floor for twenty thousand."

There was a tapping on the glass window behind his head. It continued and woke him from his dream. He moved the shade slightly and shielded his eyes from the sun, giving them time to adjust. It was Danny and Kim, both wearing a worried look on their faces. Trav motioned them toward the kitchen entrance and he slowly walked to the back door to let his friends in.

Kim moved through the open door first and gave Travis a long hug and kiss. "Are you ok?"

Dan stayed back and waited for the response, not wanting to be a bother to the couple.

"I'm fine...probably just the flu. Heck of a headache though, it was a rough go in Creative Writing."

Dan laughed and tried to interject a little humor into the conversation. "It's always a rough go in Creative Writing!"

The trio shared a laugh and took some sodas from the refrigerator.

"Did you try some Advil? Maybe you need another kiss from Miss Weston?" the girlfriend asked, trying to bring some humor and relief to the love of her life.

"Yeah, real funny...I tried the usual. Advil, cool cloth on the forehead, some soda. Just can't seem to kick the thing. Had another weird dream though."

The friends moved their gaze from Travis to each other in wonderment, then back to their friend. "Pray tell, dear friend."

"The blue house by the lake again. A party, as usual. Bruce must have been a wild man!" The trio chuckled and Travis continued with his story.

"The RAD2 was on the dock, I was about to hook it up to the pontoon. Hey, remember that guy that works with Doctor Harris? His name was Seth, right? He was in the dream and I was trying to get him to invest twenty thousand dollars into the RAD2. Ed was in the dream and he said we were going to make twenty million...twenty million, can you believe that?"

The friends remained silent but listened intently as Travis wrapped the dream up.

"I didn't get him to buy into the thing. You guys woke me up before I could sign him up."

Danny piped up apologetically. "Sorry, buddy...didn't mean to ruin your story. Hey, what do you think the dream meant?"

The dreamer shrugged and took a long sip from his can. "No idea, Dan...no idea."

Travis missed two days of school and would miss the next Thursday as well due to an appointment with Doctor Harris at the local hospital. The headaches were starting to let up but he knew he was in for bad news, he could just feel it. The young man was not in a social mood and he sat quietly, brooding the fact that nothing about this appointment could be good. He was right.

"Trav, I have some bad news. There is no good way to say this so I will just be straightforward. No more football. You're going to have to call it quits. You could have died last Friday night, you know that? You were very lucky, and I would suspect that the headaches you are having are a result of that hit in the game. You can't continue, it's too much of a risk."

He sat with his head down and tears started welling up in his eyes. He tried his best to be strong but he couldn't hold out. The tears began rolling down his cheeks.

"But, what if I just kick extra points and field goals?" His shoulders drooped and rose gently as he held as much as he could inside; he didn't want to be weak.

"I could talk to Coach, but the answer is probably no. The school will not want the liability of a possibly fatal injury."

"This isn't about the stupid school, it's about me!" he blurted out in self-pity.

"I understand, Trav, but the district is legally responsible and if something happened to you they could lose everything."

He looked her in the eyes, trying to maintain his manly composure despite the probable ending to the greatest experience of his life.

"Nothing is going to happen to me. I GUARANTEE IT! Nothing, get it?" There was an angry growl in his voice that sent a chill through her.

"You can't guarantee that, Trav. You can't guarantee that nothing is going to happen." She let him take a quiet moment to compose himself before she moved on.

"Tell me, Travis, how are your dreams?"

He appreciated the distraction from the obvious problem, settled down a little, and began talking to her about the party dream and Seth.

"Is Seth here? I want to ask him about the dream...he was in it."

A strange, puzzled expression crossed Emma Harris' face.

"Seth hasn't been here all week. Haven't you heard? Nobody seems to know where he is. It's been in the paper and on the news...everyone is extremely worried, especially me."

Chapter Twenty Two

The body was found by accident. The father and son had come up from the Twin Cities to their lake cabin to do a little hunting and were in the process of checking deer stands when it happened. The tallest stand, made of pine two by fours and plywood, stood at the end of a long, narrow swamp. A row of tall pines lined the right side and a quarter mile of woods lined the left; for all practical purposes it was a nice, secluded area that deer frequently traveled through.

The swamp was usually partially filled with water, another reason for the deer to pass along it. This year had been dry and so it was more mud than pond; the hunters hoped it wouldn't make a difference to the wildlife. They planned on bagging their usual limit of venison, a task that had never failed them before. The father climbed the twenty feet to the top of the stand carefully. Every year it seemed to be a little harder to make the ascent.

He looked down from the perch with a slight feeling of majesty, as it was a beautiful view of the area on a breathtaking morning. He looked to the far end of the basin and saw something struggling in the brush; maybe a tangled doe?

"Tommy, bring me the field glasses from the Ranger, would ya?" The teen moved quickly to the vehicle and within thirty seconds was standing next to his dad on the stand.

"I want to take a look at something, can I use them?" He reached out to his son and the boy handed over the high-powered binoculars. About one hundred and fifty yards straight out, near the end of the slew, he saw it. A large wolf was struggling with something in the brush, something buried in the muck.

"Tom, take the Ranger over there carefully and flush him out. You got your twenty-two with?" The boy nodded and worked his way down the ladder quickly. As he was climbing into the land rover, his dad gave more advice.

"Stay the hell away from that thing, it'll attack if it feels cornered. Just fire a warning shot to scare it...we don't want to kill it. There will be hell to pay if the DNR shows up and we've got a dead timber wolf."

The boy sped off and rounded the muddy area carefully, making sure to stay up on the side and not in the wet area. He moved to within twenty yards of the animal and, with a growl, the wolf took notice of the vehicle. It stopped digging and turned to face the boy.

The weapon was already loaded, all he had to do was release the safety and he was good to go. He fired the first shot over the wolves' head and the large, gray animal took off at a run. It disappeared in the opposite direction, not to be seen again. Tommy moved closer to where the animal was digging and he saw what appeared to be a head and torso.

"What is it?" the father called from across the slew, still focusing with his glasses on the far end.

"I don't know...something dead." the young man answered, moving closer.

The stench of rotting flesh hit his nostrils and he recoiled. Turning for a moment to catch his breath, he reached out with his right foot and gave the head a kick. The skull separated from the body and rolled a foot, now facing him with eyeballs missing.

He let out a scream and turned quickly away, a stream of vomit emitting from his mouth into the grass and down the front of him. He moved quickly toward the vehicle, retching every few feet and the old man on the stand realized suddenly what was going on. He focused on the round object and suddenly realized what his son had seen. A dead human.

Guilt quickly overtook the older man's mind. *I should have went over there myself to investigate. How the hell was I supposed to know a dead body was out there?"*

The teen regained his composure and drove back to the stand as quick as he could. He disembarked and stood at the base of the ladder to the tower.

"Dad. He's dead…at least I think it's a HE…I can't tell. It's real dead, nasty dead." He tried his best to avoid losing his stomach again and began to walk in circles away from the swamp.

The cell service was poor where they were and so they drove back to the cabin and called the sheriff's office. Within an hour the sheriff and coroner were arriving at the driveway to the property and two hours later the body was bagged and on its way to St. Paul for autopsy. There was no identification on the body, but the law enforcement officers had every reason to believe that they had just found Seth Emerson.

****

The phone rang as night was falling, Emma wondered who would be trying to reach her on a Saturday evening; she had no plans. *"Could be Ed. He's seems to be getting really friendly lately, maybe I'm his next conquest?"*

She laughed to herself as she picked up the phone from the kitchen table and read the identification. *"Becker County Sheriff's Office…hmm, hopefully not a harvest!"* She punched the button and answered the call.

"Hello Doc, this is Troy Haley over at Becker Sheriff's. Are you sitting down? I have something that I would rather tell you in person, but I can't get over there right now and I thought you should know before anyone else. We found Seth Emerson's body this afternoon."

Her blood ran cold and she felt light headed.

"Excuse me, did you say you found him?" The words tumbled out of her mouth, her mind was going numb and her emotions were flooding her brain. The tears started but she did her best to try and maintain her composure for the deputy.

"Yes, Emma, we found Seth partially buried in a marsh out by Buffalo Lake. I'm so sorry to have to tell you this...I know you guys worked together and were close. I'm so sorry." The line went quiet for a moment as she tried to process the information.

"Are you ok, Doc?" She nodded and then realized that he couldn't see her.

"Yes, Troy. I will be ok. Thank you for calling me so quickly."

Emma put down the phone and burst into tears, the crying consumed her whole body. She had lost patients before, but this was a colleague...more importantly a close friend. She felt more alone than ever and didn't know who to call, who to seek comfort from.

The doctor awoke the next morning in a stupor, still not believing the news she had been given the night before. She felt the urge to call the state coroner's office in St. Paul; she knew the Chief coroner, Joseph Arbuckle, personally from their many interactions of the years. There was a heavy need to know more about her friend and what may have happened to him.

The coroner's office took her call and transferred her to the doctor.

"Joe Arbuckle here." His deep voice brought up trust in her mind.

"Hi Joe, Emma Harris here...how are you?" There was a temporary pause.

"I'm probably doing much better than you, honey. His body came in late...I haven't had much time to get to it. If it's him..." She paused, confused by his last words.

"What do you mean...if it's HIM?"

"Well, the body arrived late and is really unrecognizable at this point. I don't want to get into details dear, but it is not identifiable without dental. I can't really confirm that it's Seth and I hope to hell it's not. Whoever it is...they were shot twice at close range...chest wounds...fatal."

Emma's mind was reeling. *"Who in the world would shoot Seth and why? Would they be coming for her next? If it is Seth...he was murdered?"* The coroner broke the silence.

"You ok, Em?"

"Yes, this is just a lot to take in right now."

Arbuckle was compassionate, he had always thought of her as the daughter he never had.

"I know, honey…I wish there was some way I could help. I will call you as soon as I finish the work here, ok?"

Emma Harris signed off of the phone call and her mind went into overdrive.

"It might not be Seth. Who would want to kill Seth? He never hurts anyone…was it accidental? How did they find him? Why was Troy so sure it was Seth?"

Chapter Twenty Three

Emma didn't see the email because it was tucked away with a lot of spam in her personal queue. She avoided this account because of all the bothersome offers and endless ridiculousness that was sent out across the country to everyone every day. It was from Seth and sent a shiver down her spine as she opened the contents.

She read the letter quickly the first time, then composed herself and read through it again at a more reasonable pace. She found herself building questions that were too difficult for her to solve on her own; she needed to talk to both Ed and "Bruce".

"He had it figured out...that's what killed him. What did he know that was so dangerous?"

Ed answered his phone while he was driving on the expressway across the Twin Cities and he was happy to hear from Emma. He was hoping this was a personal call that would open the door to a possible relationship; Ed was always looking for a new personal relationship.

"Ed, I got an email from my friend Seth, my friend who passed away... and I was wondering if you could help me by answering some questions?"

Her voice caught on the phrase "passed away" and she had to fight to finish the rest of the sentence without tearing up. The playboy was temporarily let down but his interest in the murder moved his mind to another level.

"What can I help you with?" he asked, hoping she might see this as a double entendre and take him up on his offer in a way he would enjoy.

"Seth starts by saying that if I am reading this letter he is probably in deep trouble, maybe dead. He knew something...he was scared of something or someone. Who would want to hurt Seth?"

Ed's mind started on the situation, he worked his way 'out of the gutter'. He didn't know what to say and so he said nothing. The doctor continued.

"I don't know who he would fear or why. He had reason to believe his safety was in jeopardy, but I don't know by who?"

Emma was quickly becoming frustrated as she was hoping he could give her information right away; this discussion seemed to be going nowhere abruptly. She decided to put him on the spot.

"What do you know about a twenty-million dollar deal concerning a device that Bruce was supposed to be selling to someone?" The line was suddenly quiet again.

"Ed, are you there?" He responded slowly, not knowing how much to disclose.

"Remember the device we were talking about with Travis? It's called the RAD2 and Bruce and I were developing it before he passed away. A company in Chicago had made a preliminary offer for it...we figured we could get twenty million for it." The line fell silent again as Emma tried to process what she had been told.

"What would Travis know about this?" she asked tentatively, hoping the kid wasn't in danger by being too close to the situation.

"Travis called me one morning a couple of weeks ago, maybe a month or more by now. He had a dream and was wondering if Bruce had accidentally killed himself by testing the RAD2 in the car he was driving. I told the kid no...no way. Travis seemed to think that the RAD2 was involved in Bruce's death. I didn't know how to handle the kid. I think you should talk to Travis, he might have some answers to your questions that I do not."

The doctor's train of thought was suddenly derailed; Travis would have to field her questions and maybe even read the email from Seth. She wasn't sure she could trust Ed and didn't want to give out any more of the information from the email than she had to. She felt more secure in pursuing answers with her young patient, she felt she could trust him and he would not harm her. Emma wasn't quite so sure about trusting Ed.

She made a quick excuse to hang up the phone, jumped into her car, and headed for the high school. If she timed it right she could pull Travis out for lunch and go through the whole email with him. Within ten minutes she was pulling into the school's parking lot, ten minutes after that she was leaving the lot with her patient seated next to her.

The local McDonald's held the greatest appeal for Travis, but Emma knew that the high school crowd who was skipping out of lunch in the cafeteria would all be headed there. It would be too busy to sit down and have a conversation, so she chose to drive across town to the local Perkins. The booths would give them the privacy necessary to talk about Seth's death and the letter that was left to her.

The restaurant was half full and commandeering a booth near the back was no problem. After ordering drinks and food, the doctor started her careful line of questioning.

"Travis, I was wondering if you could read this and figure out some of it...Seth sent it to me...it arrived in my email after he passed away and I didn't see it for a while. Spam folder."

She slowly but deliberately slid the paper copy of the email across the table and the young man opened it with a reluctant curiosity. He read it slowly, trying to digest its contents mentally, looked up for a moment or two and then read it again. He shook his head slowly and closed his eyes, not knowing what to believe.

"Travis? What do you think?"

He said nothing, he just sat still with his eyes moving between the table top and the view of the traffic passing by outside the window. She tried a different approach.

"Travis, he must have known that he might have found trouble...he talks about meeting with Troy from the Sheriff's department. Seth must have known he'd need help."

"Uh, Doc? He's not talking to the deputy about back up in case of trouble." Silence fell upon both of them as she held a puzzled expression across the table. "He's meeting WITH Troy Haley. Troy is the threat...don't you see it?"

Her jaw dropped and her eyes stared back at him with bewilderment.

"Doc, I thought this might be the case. Troy killed me...I mean Bruce. I don't know exactly how I know, but I suspected it and Seth just confirmed it."

He paused as the drinks reached the table and he took a long draw off of his Sprite.

"My dreams have been giving me more and more pieces of the puzzle. To top things off, when I went out to the blue house the first time I saw Haley with Faith and they were way too close for comfort. I realized that they had a relationship going...what I didn't figure out was that they were probably fooling around behind my back. I suspected Seth at first, but this confirms that it wasn't him. Haley was sleeping with my wife behind my back."

Doctor Harris was confused now and was struggling to follow Travis' line of reasoning.

"But I don't get it. How do you know Haley was fooling around with Faith?"

The young man was suddenly emanating an aura of a person three times his age. He seemed to be speaking as Bruce.

"It's simple. I did not kill myself...on purpose or by accident. I couldn't control the car because someone hooked up the RAD2 to the computer system. The RAD2 had been missing for over a week. I didn't kill myself, someone killed me. Now the question is why? Simple. If someone was fooling around with Faith they might want me gone. Faith might want me dead for the insurance money. Ed might want me dead so that he could take my half of the cash from the Chicago deal. Hell, Seth knew enough about the deal to where he might have stolen the RAD and wanted me dead. There's plenty of people who benefit if I am gone."

He fell quiet for a minute as the food arrived and he shook his head back and forth slowly. Emma Harris felt very sorry for him at that moment.

"You know though, Doc, Seth didn't kill me. He had an alibi…he was with you. Also, he wouldn't know how to hook up the RAD2…whoever killed me had to hook it up. I didn't have it hooked to the car. Also, whoever killed me had taken the RAD over a week before. They had to know what it was, where it was, and how to hook it up."

Emma worked within his line of reasoning and asked "Who would know how to hook it up? Think of everyone."

Travis took a couple of bites from his burger and chewed while deep in thought.

"Faith would have known what it was, where it was, but could never hook it up. She never paid much attention to it, she paid much more attention to her booze and her tan."

He ate more of his lunch while thinking of all the possibilities and quickly realized there weren't many people who could hook it up.

"Carl Avery down in Minneapolis could hook it up and operate it. He was the chief designer and he had a staff of people who helped him put it together. There's no motive there, though. If anything, he would have wanted me alive because I was making the pitch to sell it and he stood to make a lot of money on the patent rights. A small percent of every RAD2 sold. He needed me too much to kill me. Other than him, the only people who could hook it up and run it were myself and Ed. Ed would never kill me."

****

Emma Harris was now scared of Ed Payne; according to Travis he was the only one who could hook up the remote control to the car. She had probably confided too much in him and now she might be a target in the same sense as Seth had been. Sitting at her desk as the afternoon wound down, she started doodling on a note pad with a pencil and she began to work through the scenario by talking to herself softly.

"Ed Payne is the only person who could hook up the system, other than Bruce and some technician in the cities. Bruce didn't kill himself. What about the crash scene? What did Seth know that I didn't? I have to go back to the reports and the people on the scene to find out where the RAD2 was...was it even there? What about Troy Haley? Travis seems pretty sure there was an affair between the cop and Faith? I have to go back to the scene or records and figure out what happened that night."

First thing the next morning, the doctor went over to the high school to ask Travis a few more questions. She checked in at the front office and was told by the attendance secretary that her patient was absent for the day; he hadn't reported to first or second hour. She then drove the half mile to his house and rang the doorbell.

There was no answer at the front door. Mrs. Adamson was most certainly at work; the doctor made her way to the back of the house and peeked in the young man's window. She could see Travis laying on his bed, sound asleep.

Travis had heard the doorbell and began to move very slowly from his bed. His head felt like it was exploding and he could barely open his eyes. He turned toward the irritating light from the bedroom window and he jumped when he saw her. The good doctor was peeking in at him. After a momentary fright, he smiled and moved to the kitchen door to let her in.

"Travis, how come you are not at school?" Emma asked with genuine concern. The young man moved very slowly while cradling his head in his hands.

"My head feels like it's going to explode...I can hardly open my eyes...it hurts so bad." He laid back down on his bed in the darkened room and turned away from the window.

"Trav...when you hurt this bad you have to call me. This is not good. We should head over to the hospital and get you something for the pain."

He wasn't about to argue, he felt horrible and the headaches were becoming an almost daily occurrence. They made the five-minute drive to the hospital and he was checked into a comfortable room and given proper pain medication. Doctor Harris felt better knowing that he was in a secure location and could manage his discomfort; she made a promise to herself to re-visit in the early evening.

The doctor returned to find her patient in much better spirits; the pain was pretty much gone. Mrs. Adamson was sitting next to his bed with considerable concern on her mind. There wasn't much that Emma Harris could do to console her or put her mind at rest.

The pain episodes were troubling to the doctor; in her past cases this had never happened this late into the transplant process. The concussion sustained during football probably had much to do with the problem, but she wasn't completely convinced that this was the fact. After settling in with some small talk, Emma decided to pursue her reasoning with a few questions.

"Travis, I was thinking. When we were having lunch yesterday, you said that Troy Haley was a suspect in Bruce's murder. You even suspected him of having an affair with your wife. Why would you say that?"

The young man shook his head with a strange smile on his face. Both women suddenly felt Bruce's presence in room.

"I always suspected that Faith was cheating on me...she hung around with other men a little too closely, a little too much affection and flirting. I know Ed had the hots for her, but seeing her with Haley when I went out there just looked too real."

He stopped for a moment and then continued with his thought process. The mother and doctor sat still with a quiet, yet intense interest.

"By getting me out of the way, he could have her. The insurance money would be a great benefit as well for both of them. He watched me run the remote device, he even piloted it one night when we had a big party at the lake home. Seth was there, he was playing with it too. Ed could hook it up, I could hook it up, but I would bet you dimes to dollars that Haley could do it too. Especially if he stole it and took it to a mechanic in town...it's not the most complicated device in the world to work with."

Emma's mind suddenly sprang to life even though she remained still.

"Damn it, how come I didn't think of that? The mechanic shops in town that would work with the Sheriff's office...they have their own mechanic and garage outside of town. The car itself...where is the wreck? Could a mechanic tell me if this thing was hooked up? Where is the RAD2 now? Where did it go after the crash? At the site? Was it even there? Who could have taken it?"

Emma's mind was racing as she said goodbye to Travis quickly; her mind was racing out of control and she had to sit down and process what she was thinking. The doctor quickly made her way to the nurse's station in the hallway, grabbed some paper and a pen, and wrote down everything that ran through her mind. Tomorrow would be a very busy day; she had a lot of leads to pursue.

Chapter Twenty Four

Emma knew she had to get the records of the crash but could not trust Troy Haley. She knew one person who could keep a secret and have access to the information she needed; she stopped over to the Sheriff's office and visited Dottie Green, the front office secretary and main dispatcher for the county.

"Hi Dottie, how are you?" the doctor greeted in the friendliest way she knew.

"I'm good sweetie, what brings you by here?"

The elderly clerk seemed to call everyone 'sweetie' and she had taken a special liking to the female doctor who reminded her of a younger version of herself. Emma leaned in and smiled as she made her request.

"I was wondering if you could do me a favor? I need some records of a crash a while ago that I worked on...strictly legal stuff, no big deal."

The clerk smiled and made her suggestion.

"Would you like to talk to Sheriff Reynolds or Troy Haley?"

Emma knew that either one would be a problem and so she worked her way around that idea.

"You know, Dottie, I wouldn't want to bother them. Could you just print me a copy of the accident report so I could look at it in my office?" Ms. Green had a look of concern on her face for a moment.

"You know, Doc, we aren't supposed to give out reports. But for you I can make an exception, with you being the doctor on the scene, right?"

A smile returned to both of the ladies' faces and Doctor Harris made reference to the right files.

"I need the report for the accident that Bruce Nickel passed away in."

"Oh, my! I remember that, how sad, huh? He seemed like such a nice guy."

Emma nodded and within five minutes she was walking to her car with a copy of the official county report on the accident.

After settling into her car, she drove three blocks to a secluded little park in the middle of town and stopped to read the contents of the manila folder. She found what she was looking for and her mind flashed to the location of the salvage yard where the car was dumped after the accident in Richwood.

"Interesting, they towed Bruce's car to Little Floyd Lake Road. Andresen's Salvage. Think I better take a trip out there." She was speaking aloud to no one but herself and she put the car into gear and started out of town to the yard.

The small town gave way to a beautiful, rural countryside and ten miles later she was turning off the main road onto an access road that led around a pretty lake. Another mile left the lake in her rearview mirror and suddenly she was passing a huge plat of wrecked vehicles. Emma found the dirt driveway and recognized the rusty, tin building that had seen too many Minnesota winters.

Pulling up to an open dirt space in front of the establishment Emma got out and cautiously went inside. There were tires and auto parts strewn throughout the building and an older gentleman with no hair was sitting casually on a stool, reading the newspaper.

"Harold! How's my favorite old man?" Her greeting was sincerely and the old guy wore a smile from ear to ear.

"Doing wonderful, Doc! What in the world brings you way out here?" She laughed softly and replied "I missed you at the diner Tuesday morning!"

He laughed a genuine laugh, happy to have a visitor in this remote area. The fact that she was half his age and very attractive also pleased him.

"Harold, I need a bit of a favor. I have to take a look at a vehicle that was brought in some time ago. It was towed from a terrible accident north of here, up by Richwood."

He nodded, turned from his newspaper, and looked out toward the yard.

"We get a few from Richwood...every so often. They drive too damn fast up there."

"The car I'm looking for was in the Bruce Nickel accident about two years ago...give or take. Would you have that car on hand?" She slid the report across the counter top to Harold and he looked at the vehicle description.

"Yeah, I got it yet. Probably out on the back forty. There wasn't much to salvage if I remember correctly and I haven't hauled scrap from here in a long time...can't get a good price for it. Not worth the bother right now."

He stood up slowly and shuffled toward the back door and the huge expanse of broken-down autos. Emma couldn't tell if the creaking was from the old, wooden floor or the old man's bones.

"C'mon, follow me and we'll go take a look."

The old man shuffled over to a beat-up golf cart and motioned for Emma to slide in. He drove slowly, weaving his way between old autos and piles of metal and rubber. The bumpy roadway was annoying for the doctor, she kept bouncing and teetering on the edge of the cart.

"You can use your seat belt if you'd like." She shot the old man a worried smile and declined.

They drove out to where the weeds got higher and the piles of rubble diminished; now it was just old cars. It was unseasonably warm for mid- November and Emma enjoyed the warmth of the sun on her face. It wouldn't be long before the snow would fly.

As they neared a large, leafless oak tree she saw it...the black sedan with the front end pushed in. Harold pulled the cart up next to it and pointed.

"Is this what you're looking for?"

She looked at the first page of the file and noted the license plate. The car description and plate numbers matched.

"This is it, Harold. Can we take a closer look?" He smiled at the younger woman in a fatherly manner.

"Sure, dear."

The doctor found herself averting her eyes from the inside of the car; she could sense Bruce's presence and remembered the crash scene too vividly.

"Can we look at the engine?"

The old man looked to her and then pried back the remnants of the hood, noting that there wasn't much left.

"What are you looking for? It's just an old engine with damage. He hit the biggest fuckin' tree in the county. Oh, sorry dear."

Harold paused and lowered his gaze toward the ground, embarrassed that he had cussed in front of a woman. Emma didn't pay any attention to the faux paus. The old man continued on.

"I don't think I can get much for it...might send the whole thing out when the salvage buyers show next month."

"Harold, where is the computer stuff on one of these things?" The old man turned to her and wondered aloud why she wanted that.

"I'm looking for a remote device that would have been left on this thing. A black box about this big." She spread her hands apart and gave him a rough dimension of the thing she was looking for.

"This thing would be hooked into the electrical system and computer for the car...you would be able to drive the car with a remote-control device."

The old man was even more puzzled now, he had no idea what she was talking about.

"I don't know what you're looking for, never heard of it." He shook his head emphatically to stress his confusion.

"Tell you what, Harold. Could you take a look and see if anything looks out of the ordinary with the electrical or computer systems?" The old man looked at the doctor, then the car, then back to the doctor.

"I can try."

The salvage owner moved around to the passenger side of the wreck and worked to open the front door. With substantial effort the metal gave way and the door screeched open. He slowly crept under the dash on the passenger side and moved to open the electrical box, which was already loose. Three wires were sticking out and hanging on a black piece of plastic which had obviously been torn away from something else.

"This is weird...it's not supposed to be here." The old man pulled the wires free and stood up, holding them towards Emma. "Don't know what this is...do you?"

The doctor smiled, realizing that they may have found the proverbial 'smoking gun'.

"Harold, that's what I was telling you about." He turned to her with another question.

"This doesn't look anything like what you just described, how do you know what it is?" She smiled back at the elderly gentleman.

"It's not the whole device. Someone has the rest of it, this was just left when they ripped it out at the accident scene."

He smiled with realization that she knew what she was talking about.

"Where would the computer be on this thing?" Harold moved into the engine compartment on the same side of the car and found a disconnected wire running through the firewall to the passenger compartment.

"Don't know what this is either, but I'm betting you do!" He stepped back as she moved around the car to his side and pulled out her cellphone.

"We can leave the wire, but I'm going to take a picture."

They hopped back into the golf cart and headed back to the shop. The ride back didn't seem nearly as harrowing because Emma had found what she was looking for. The trip was a success and she was excited. Her mind was no longer on her safety, but instead was on what she would have do next. When they returned to the tin building, she made a final request.

"Harold, could you do me a huge favor? Do not sell off that car just yet. Do not tell anyone I was here or what we found…not even the police, especially the Sheriff's department. This will be our little secret. If I have to, I will even buy the wreck out there from you."

The old man knew something was up, but he was thrilled to be in the midst of something big. With a reassuring grin on his weathered face, he made her smile.

"You don't have to worry, dear, I won't tell a soul. Don't worry about the car. I won't do anything with it until you tell me too and you don't have to buy it from me. This will be our little secret…just like you said."

She took the chunk of wires off of the countertop, turned to the old man and gave him a heartfelt embrace, then headed out to her car and back to town.

****

Dr. Harris was sitting at the kitchen table with Sylvia Adamson when Travis walked in the front door and through the house towards them. She could hear his backpack hit the floor at the entrance to his room and then he sauntered in with Kim, both looking for something good to cure their hunger. Greetings were exchanged in haste, as the young kids were quick to rummage through the fridge and pantry. The couple joined the older pair at the kitchen table with their sodas and chips.

After engaging the teenagers in small talk that revolved around their school day, Emma changed the subject and sprang the question on Travis.

"Say Trav, you wouldn't happen to know what this is, would you?" She took the bundle of plastic and wires from her carry bag on the floor next to her and placed it on the table in front of him. He looked at it quizzically and then picked it up for closer examination. The room was quiet as he inspected the wires one by one.

"This is the wire connection for power to the RAD2. Someone damaged it...they broke this piece off from the box. Where did you get this?" A heavy silence returned to the table as Emma struggled to present her findings.

"I got this from Bruce's car. I went to the salvage yard and saw the sedan. This was in the front seat, under the dash...my friend Harold helped me with it. Are you alright?"

The young man sat quietly, showing no emotion on his face.

"I didn't imagine it. I couldn't control the car. I was murdered." He sounded like Bruce now and everyone watched him with care, not quite knowing how to act or what to say.

"That's right, Travis, it certainly looks like Bruce was murdered."

Chapter Twenty Five

"Whoever killed me knew how to hook the device up and operate it...I kind of figured that, but now I KNOW it. It's time to find them and take them down for good...this won't go unsolved."

The young man was speaking with conviction and Emma found herself thrilled with the prospect of moving toward bringing the case to a close and handing down justice to someone who deserved it. She was as fired up as Travis was.

"It's Troy Haley... I'm pretty sure he killed me. The motive is there and the knowledge of the device is there...has to be him. All we have to do is find the other portion of the RAD2, the main box...it will be missing this piece." He held up the remnants that the doctor had presented to him moments before.

"We will get him as soon as we find the rest of the RAD2."

****

The thought of Troy Haley murdering Bruce had kept Travis up for most of the night. He just couldn't find a way to get the events of the day out of his mind, it seemed that so much was suddenly happening and his headaches were getting worse. He finally drifted off to sleep after two in the morning.

The dream entered his mind almost immediately and it was very vivid. Bruce was driving into Twin Lakes on Roosevelt road when the squad car suddenly crept up behind him and hit its lights. He cursed to himself and pulled over on the edge of the city limits. This was a known speed trap where the limit went from forty-five to thirty miles per hour; he should have known better as he had been busted here before.

Officer Haley stepped out of the car. Bruce could see him in his rearview mirror and he felt happy because he knew he would probably get away with a warning. The deputy stepped up to the driver's window and smiled right away.

"Hi Bruce, where you going in such a hurry?" Bruce returned the smile.

"Sorry Troy, I always seem to forget the speed change back there." The deputy nodded and let the driver continue.

"I'm headed into town to Bailey's auto repair. I'm going to have them install something on my car." Deputy Haley scanned the contents of the car and focused on the black box sitting on the front seat.

"What's that?" he asked with genuine curiosity. Bruce turned toward the passenger seat and realized what the question focused on.

"This is the remote that I'm going to have installed. It's a prototype that I have been trying to market in the Cities and if I'm successful, I could make one hell of a lot of money with it!"

Haley chuckled back at Bruce, he was bored and this was much better than sitting on a side street speed-trapping everyone who drove by.

"Hey, I'm off work in fifteen minutes. Can I come over and watch them put that thing on your car. It looks really cool. Is that the gizmo that you had on your boat at the party last month?"

Bruce was flattered that the young officer would be interested in his work. He also knew that he wouldn't be getting a ticket if he complied with Haley.

"Tell you what. Finish your shift and drive over to Bailey's, you can help put it on. Then maybe we can run over to the fairgrounds and try the thing out, ok?"

Travis awoke from the dream in a sweat, he was mentally shaken and felt like he was going to vomit. "Son of a bitch! That bastard watched me hook up the RAD2 !"

He rolled off the side of his bed and grabbed at his backpack. Finding a pencil and notebook in the overfilled satchel, he turned on his bedside lamp and spent an adequate amount of time writing down every detail he could remember from his dream. It was Bruce's dream, a remembrance of an event he had lived.

The young man made two more notes at the bottom of the page and then put the book on his nightstand.

"Tell Dr. Harris about the dream."

The last memo was a single line that he knew was important to follow up on.

"Break into Troy Haley's place and find the RAD2."

Chapter Twenty Six

He sauntered into the diner a tad over six foot four and weighed something well north of two hundred and sixty pounds. Everyone took notice when John Buffalo walked into a room; he commanded the attention of all. Emma had watched him from the time he pulled into the snowy parking lot until he walked to the register and she couldn't take her eyes off him. After getting directions from the young lady behind the counter, he turned toward the doctor and flashed a big smile.

He carried his wide brimmed hat in his hands as he approached her booth and, as intimidating as he seemed, she felt extremely secure in his presence. An elderly couple from the neighboring table greeted him and he exchanged pleasantries with them in a genuine manner. If there was one thing that stood out about him besides his enormous size it was his genuine manner.

"You must be Doctor Harris." He stated in a strong but friendly voice. Emma smiled and held out her hand.

"Yes, please call me Emma." The patrolman took her hand gently in his and held it a moment longer than was customary. She didn't mind.

"Harold told me who you were but he sure didn't tell me how lovely you are!" The statement held her momentarily speechless and all she could manage was a pretty smile.

"May I join you for a little breakfast?"

She nodded with a continuous smile and moved her coffee close as he slid into the booth.

"Harold says you are the most upstanding, trustworthy lawman he knows. That's high praise from someone like Harold." The big man smiled and let out a gentle laugh.

"Harold gives me way too much credit!" He was flattered by the comment though and Emma knew she had charmed him.

There was a magic chemistry at the table and both of them felt it simultaneously. The conversation centered on small talk for the first couple of minutes and it was effortless for Emma. She hadn't struck up a liking to a man like John for a long time.

"My gosh, he's charming! I hope he feels the same about me!"

The doctor wanted to know more, much more about the lawman sitting across from her. After placing their breakfast order and indulging in hot coffee, Emma got to the point with her new friend.

"Harold suggested that I talk with you concerning a case from a couple of years ago. He said you could be trusted and could keep a secret." The big man nodded and his curiosity was now aroused.

"I'm looking into an accident from a couple of years ago that involved a wealthy man over in Richwood who passed away. Over on County 34 by the church on Buffalo Lake."

John nodded and recognized the case instantly. "I remember. I don't usually work that area...I'm usually up north on the Rez."

The Rez was the White Earth Native American Reservation, about fifteen miles to the north of the area that Emma was talking about.

"I tend to handle the problems up there. I'm Native American myself and know pretty much everyone." There was a slight braggadocio to his tone, he was proud of his heritage and his diplomacy on the reservation. John continued in his strong but gentlemanly manner.

"Why wouldn't you talk to the officers that handled the call? I'm guessing Becker county had that one to themselves." The doctor nodded, her eyes still locked with his in admiration.

"They had it. The problem is one of the deputies might have been in on the accident." He was puzzled now and his expression changed but still held her fascination.

"What do you mean by 'in on it'?" Emma then took the next ten minutes, stopping only for the arrival of the food, to explain the whole situation and how Troy Haley was the main suspect.

"I get it…I get it. But you are telling me that this kid has the brain from the dead guy in his head and he's dreaming all this shit up? Oh, sorry…excuse me."

The big man was blushing now, realizing that he had used inappropriate language in front of this lovely lady. Emma found him cute and sexy at the same time. John Buffalo shook his head slowly and, with a look of puzzlement and slight disbelief, continued on.

"He's dreaming this stuff up and getting messages from the dead guy? No offense, but this seems a little far-fetched to me…not that I doubt you, but it is a little weird…you know?" She smiled and her infatuation doubled on the spot as she watched him struggle with the story she had presented.

"That's exactly what's happening, its why we need help from someone like you…someone who knows law enforcement and the legal system. Someone on the inside. Would you be able to help us out with this?"

She used her coy voice, hoping that she could persuade him with cuteness. *Good lord, I'm in my mid-thirties and I'm cooing like a high school girl!* Her charm worked its magic on the big man.

"Normally I would probably say no and think you were CRAZY!" He twirled his index finger near his temple, round and round for effect. Then he cast a wide, beaming smile upon her. "But you are too adorable to say no to...count me in."

****

Bitter cold from the arctic north brought in the Thanksgiving break at Twin Lakes High School and Travis was glad for the holiday as he had already been missing two to three days of school per week. The headaches were getting worse and his anxiety was increasing as he thought about Troy Haley killing him. Bruce was in his head almost constantly and the thoughts were getting louder; he was forgetting who the young Travis was.

He woke up from a deep sleep and groggily looked out his bedroom window at the overcast day. Large, white flakes were coming down and he dreaded the idea of having to shovel the driveway next to his house. He listened and heard only the furnace churning out the heated air; his mom was already at work downtown. Shaking his head lightly to clear the cobwebs from his brain, he had a strange feeling that he should have remembered his dream from the night before.

He moved much too slow for a boy his age, the heavy steps he took to the kitchen were the product of the old man inside him. He dug out his favorite cereal from the side pantry, grabbed milk from the refrigerator, and armed himself with a large bowl and a spoon. That was one side he couldn't ignore; the young man in him was famished. Pouring a heaping bowl of sugary goodness, he dug in with gusto and began to wake up.

Travis had the sudden, overwhelming urge to call up Ed in the cities. Not knowing why or what to say, he just felt that it was necessary and so he dialed up his old friend.

"Ed Payne."

Travis smiled, realizing that the old man was too busy to answer the phone as he sounded annoyed.

"Hey old man, why don't you get to work, huh? Get your hands out of your pants!"

The old man laughed with gusto, recognizing Travis' voice right away.

"You should talk...that's a young man's game...I get some."

Their dirty repartee turned more serious after a minute and Travis began to explain the situation with Troy Haley.

"Ed, I KNOW he killed me...I can just feel it, deep down. He had the motive and he saw me install the RAD2. He did it to get rid of me, to get Faith, to get the insurance money, and to sell the RAD2 with you. Nobody would suspect him."

"You know kid, I think you're on to something. He was always kind of snooping around and he sure had a thing for Faith. If he saw you install the RAD, it would explain a lot. The damn thing was missing for a week before the crash...damn it, I'll bet he had it."

Travis was nodding confidently as he took another spoonful of cereal, happy that Ed could see the reasoning that he had figured out.

"So, what should we do?" the young man asked, eager to pursue and apprehend his killer.

"Sit still with this for a bit. I have to figure a couple of things out on my end. We will need proof beyond a doubt to catch him…the damn crime is over two years old. Give me a couple of days to talk to some friends on my end and we will move on Haley when the time is right."

The old man was buying precious time to figure the situation out and Travis agreed to wait for a couple of days.

Travis punched off the cell phone carefully and set it on the table. Moving to the bathroom, he took off his pajamas and jumped into a hot shower. The warmth felt good on his skull and he lathered up quickly. The steam permeated his body and the world seemed like a wonderful place; he stood in the hot stream of water longer than he should have, but he felt he deserved it. Bruce was going to catch his killer.

The snow stopped falling as he looked out the small bathroom window. Travis was relieved to see that there wasn't much more than a half inch of white stuff on the driveway and so he wouldn't be expected to shovel. It would be a great day to relax with video games or his guitar. His quiet, relaxing world was interrupted by a knock on the door.

He pulled his pajama pants on quickly and wrapped the damp towel across his shoulders while moving toward the front door. Feeling he was decent, he opened the door and the cold air hit him like a wave, making him shiver. Doctor Harris was standing on the front step with one of the largest cops that Travis had ever seen behind her. He was suddenly scared. Travis was at a loss for words, he just stood in the open doorway with his mouth agape.

"C'mon kid, you going to let us in? It's cold out here!" Emma was laughing while looking at this astonished expression. Travis stepped back and allowed them to enter the warmth of the living room.

"Travis Adamson meet John Buffalo...Officer Buffalo, this is Travis." The two men exchanged a manly handshake and Travis took a moment to note that his hand was completely engulfed by the cops' paw.

"Dang, you are one BIG dude!" The kid was laughing as he stated the obvious.

This broke the ice and Travis left the two guests for a minute in his living room while he ran off to put on some jeans and a sweatshirt. They re-gathered in the kitchen at the alcove table that offered natural light and a pleasant view of the backyard.

"Officer Buffalo has been doing some detective work for us concerning Troy Haley. You might not believe what he seems to have found." Emma turned the discussion over to her new boyfriend and the officer carefully began to assess his findings.

"I took a look at the remnants of the remote control that was left in the sedan...if we find the other half we will be well on our way to pinning this on the killer."

Travis was a little impatient, he was quick to point out that what John Buffalo thought was very obvious.

"We already know that Troy Haley is the killer. I already know that finding the remote will prove his guilt." The large man across the table smiled as he recognized the impatient, know it all temperament of the youth.

"I found something else though." The officer looked from the young man to the doctor, nodded, and continued.

"I checked the 911 call and response records. I know everyone that showed up on the scene and the time that they got there. I can even tell where they came from when the call came in. Troy Haley was not the first responder, in fact he was the third car on the scene and he arrived almost five minutes after the first squad."

Travis was confused.

"That can't be. He would have had to drive the car with the remote and then remove it after the crash. He had to be the first, or else he was really sneaky when it came to taking the RAD2 out of the car."

John Buffalo smiled as he admired the way Travis was thinking. The young man was using logic as he was working his way through the sequence of the crash.

"What do you think the odds are that Troy Haley drove the car, crashed it killing Bruce, then took the remote before anyone showed up on the scene?" There was no answer at the table, only shrugs and curious looks.

"Troy was speed trapping on Roosevelt Road, at the edge of town...he was too far away to run a remote. He heard the crash call as he was writing a ticket and he let the guy off with a warning so that he could respond."

"Let me get this straight... you're saying that Troy didn't kill me...I mean Bruce?"

The young man was somewhat flustered with this news, it threw his idea out the window.

"Yes. According to the response records there is no way that Troy killed you...I mean Bruce."

Travis looked down at the table top and shook his head, his headache was starting to return and his frustration was becoming visible in his body language.

"Who killed me then?" he asked in a weak voice, feeling defeated.

"I don't know kid, I don't know. But you can damn well bet that we will catch them...we're going to solve this thing."

The big man looked from the young man to the doctor and locked eyes with her. She felt assured that he was the right man for this case and hopefully the right man for her.

Chapter Twenty Seven

"Travis, it's Ed. I've been thinking and talking to a few friends down here who work in law enforcement. We have to find the RAD2...whoever has it is guilty. I think you should go out to the house on Buffalo Lake and check the garage. Bruce always had the thing in there. If Faith or Troy was trying to kill you, and I don't think its Faith, then the remote should be there. I just have a really strong feeling on this one."

Travis was frustrated as he had already pursued this with his friends.

"Ed, I've already been out there...twice. The last time I was there I almost got caught. The crazy bitch fired a pistol at me and damn near hit me. I do not want to go back...I think it's too dangerous." There was a silent pause on the line, Travis could hear his old friend breathing in a frustrated manner.

"Trav, just do this for me...do it for Bruce. I just have this feeling, just something that I KNOW...the RAD2 has to be there. I'm pretty sure that Faith is down here in the cities...you will be safe. Please check it one more time…please?" Ed was pleading for him to try again and he didn't want to let the old friend down.

"Tell you what, Ed. I will go out there one more time, but only one more time. She sees me out there and I'll be arrested or killed. This is not good! One more time."

The old man whispered his thanks and hung up.

The high school sleuth placed his next call to his best friend.

"Danny, old boy…want to stir up a little trouble?" he said with a sly grin.

"Uh, oh. What are you about to do now?" His friend had learned to be tentative with him, as Travis had a way of digging up trouble.

"Let's go back out to Bruce's blue house."

Danny started coughing or choking on the other end of the line.

"ARE YOU NUTS?! WE ALMOST GOT KILLED OUT THERE LAST TIME, DON'T YOU REMEMBER?!"

A half hour later the boys pulled away from the curb in front of Travis' house and slowly headed toward the middle of town. Dan was driving slowly, wondering to himself why he was listening to Travis and trying something that sounded like certain trouble.

"Let's make a stop somewhere else first. Drive over to Third Avenue, 128 Third." Danny looked across at his friend.

"Why?! Where are we going?" He didn't like the look on Travis' face.

"We have to pay a little visit to Troy Haley's house first. I want to see if the RAD2 is there." The truck pulled over to the curb abruptly.

"You have to be kidding. Now we are going to break into a police officer's house? Seriously? This is a joke, right?"

"No joke, buddy. We have to make sure he doesn't have the RAD2. Let's just check his garage. He isn't going to put the thing in his house...he'll put it in the garage." The truck began to move slowly.

"You are going to get both of us killed. I can see it now. Two high schoolers shot dead by law enforcement after breaking and entering and attempted theft!"

Travis laughed, trying to break the tension. "It will not be attempted theft...I can't steal something I already own!"

They pulled up to the curb at 128 Third and looked at the small, white bungalow that had to be pushing one-hundred years old.

"Guess they don't pay deputies very well, huh?" Danny observed quietly.

"He doesn't have much of a house, but he has quite the girlfriend. Remember, he's doing Faith."

Both the boys laughed at the off-color statement and realized that they were jealous of the cop. They looked around at the neighboring houses and, seeing no one, they moved up to the door of 128.

Travis knocked, not knowing what he was going to say if Troy came to the door. He could always make up some crap about a fundraiser for football or something. With a job or girlfriend to keep him busy, it was a good bet he wasn't home. There was no answer and so they moved to the back door and tried again. Again, nothing.

"Let's check out his garage."

They tried the small garage door on the side and it opened right away. Inside was a squad car for Becker county.

"Shit! He might be home!" Dan whispered with alarm.

"No way. He would have answered the door. He's probably out in another car. Let's go in for a second."

The boys made their way inside and did a quick once over of the tool bench and shelving. No RAD2. The sound they heard behind them made them freeze. It was a bullet being jacked into the chamber of a gun.

"You boys lost?" They turned slowly to face Troy Haley and his weapon.

"One is likely to get blown to bits while stealing from a man's garage. What the hell are you two doing here?"

Dan was on the verge of fainting, he couldn't utter a sound. Travis took the lead and hoped he wouldn't get shot.

"We thought we were in a friend's garage...we didn't take anything, seriously. Toby lives here, right? 128 Fourth Avenue." He looked confused and defeated.

"Hey, brain surgeon...this is 128 Third and I'm a cop. Suppose I had better take you in. Let's go." He waved the weapon towards the squad car and the boys started to move.

"Stop!" He pointed the gun at them again. "Tell you what. You don't want to go in and frankly, I don't want to haul your sorry asses in either. Get out of my garage and don't come back...EVER, YOU HEAR?!"

"Yes sir, sorry about the mix up."

Both boys passed the cop and ran out the door. They could hear Troy Haley laughing inside the garage but they didn't want to stop and join him. Down the driveway and across the street they ran, both scared out of their wits. They jumped into the truck and sped to the corner, barely stopping at the stop sign. It was a good two minutes before either of them said a word. Then Travis started laughing.

"What's so damn funny, numb nuts?!" his friend shouted in a high-pitched squeak, still freaking out from the encounter with the deputy. Travis continued laughing during his reply.

"He wasn't going to shoot us, he was just trying to scare us...to mess with us. He wasn't ever going to fire a shot." Dan's feelings gyrated between hurt and scared.

"That was NOT FUNNY! None of this is funny."

Travis stopped laughing and consoled his friend. "Don't worry, we have luck on our side."

A half hour later they were on their way to the blue house in Danny's pickup truck and all the driver could do was shake his head and moan.

"Geez, give it a rest, huh? Ed says she's not even home...come on, it will not take very long. One quick look in the garage to shut Ed up and we are on our way out of there." Dan looked across at his friend and just mumbled and shook his head some more.

They drove past the property slowly, looking for any signs of recent occupancy. The large, dark green garbage containers were tipped over at the end of the driveway, the result of a hungry bear or raccoon.

"Park back up by the church and we'll walk down, it will be less suspicious." They parked and walked the quarter mile to the house, making their way to the back deck.

"Shit, she's got the alarm set...we must have freaked her out last time. Grab the key over there under the pot and I'll punch in the code."

They opened the single door with the key and the alarm began to chirp; they had about a minute to disarm the system or it would howl and the police would be on the way.

"I hope she didn't change the code or we are in deep shit!"

Travis punched the numbers to the day, month, and year of their wedding and the system went silent.

"Thank you, Bruce." he whispered loud enough for Dan to hear. They moved through the familiar house and it felt strangely cold. Travis went to the thermostat in the kitchen and noted the 59 degree temperature.

"She hasn't been here in a long time. She set the 'stat for 59 like we would always do when we closed this place up for the winter." He moved over to the fridge and opened the swinging door.

"Empty. She's gone for the winter."

They toured the house carefully as they didn't want to be detected. Travis paused in the bedroom and pocketed a perfume bottle of Faith's. The garage was the final stop and Travis saw it right away. Sitting on the third shelf next to his tool bench was the RAD2, missing wires and all. The young man went cold inside and openly shivered, realizing that he had just found the device that led to Bruce's demise.

"Go get the truck and I'll meet you out front...DO NOT pull into the driveway, I will come to the road."

Dan headed back through the house and out the door. Travis sat down on the step that led from the house to the garage and thought quietly for a moment.

"Damn it, there's no way he did it. Did Faith kill me? She couldn't hook it up. Did Troy hook it up and have Faith kill me? Maybe. Shit. He killed me...I can't believe it."

Travis had tears streaming down his face as he closed up the garage and house, carrying the RAD2 in his left hand. He made a bee line for the truck and Dan noticed his distress.

The friend said nothing, partially out of pity and partially out of confusion. They drove in silence and reached the city limits as the sun was going down. Setting the RAD2 on his kitchen table, Travis called Emma and told her to bring Big John.

Chapter Twenty Eight

"Look, we don't know for sure, but this looks pretty cut and dried." Officer Buffalo had listened to Travis and had gone over all the facts in the case. "It is probably 75/25 that Ed killed Bruce. On the other hand, I wouldn't rule out Troy and Faith...love can make people do some awfully crazy shit. Oh, sorry dear." He turned to Emma with an embarrassed look. She smiled with a smirk as she had heard much worse in her time.

"I have something else here that may be of interest to us. A note was sent into the sheriff's office and the boss asked me about it. It states that a call was made to our office around the time that Seth Emerson disappeared. It also says that the call came from Seth and was answered by a deputy. Whoever wrote the note says that they intercepted the call and that they can prove that the deputy was supposed to meet with Seth. It kind of looks like we might have the person who killed Seth serving in our department."

With eyes wide, Travis couldn't remain silent. "I knew it!" He banged his open palms on the table with conviction. "Troy killed Seth because he must have known something about Bruce's death. I knew it!"

Officer Buffalo was moving slower, as he wasn't quite as sure as the young man. "I don't know...we don't even know who took the call, much less if they met with Seth. Also, we have no idea who left this note...I just can't be so sure."

"What do you mean? We know there was a motive and we know that Troy could install and operate the system. Now we have him killing someone who could implicate him...what else do we need? He's GUILTY! Let's get him!"

The officer looked from Travis to Doctor Harris and shook his head slowly. "We don't have enough to convict, probably not enough to even make the charges stick."

Something deep in Travis' mind told him that John was right and the next thought he had sent a shiver down his spine.

****

Big John had the afternoon off, he had just completed a long overnight shift on the reservation but didn't feel tired yet. He faced this problem often; he would work a long stint and then be too tired to sleep; then he would get a jolt of energy.

Not ready to drive north to his home in Ogema, he decided to do a little detective work for Emma. She was on his mind a lot lately and he knew he should move on her. Being a few years beyond his fortieth birthday but still being young at heart, he knew deep down that time was becoming more precious.

He wanted to be her hero. Grabbing a couple of pieces of printer paper from the copy room, he settled down in an empty office with a pen and began to draw the scenario he was studying. After about ten minutes of brainstorming and drawing arrows and circles, he stopped and smiled.

"The call to Troy that came in by way of the dispatcher...Troy had to be covering the desk. It wouldn't be 911 because the caller wouldn't know he was manning the post. It had to be the regular line. Whoever made that call could be location traced from the regular line."

With all the charm he could muster, the officer moved quickly to the secretary at the front desk.

"Hi Dottie, I have a favor to ask you." The receptionist was smiling as she gave him a reply he didn't expect.

"Rumor has it that a handsome officer from up on the Rez was seen with a very attractive doctor at a certain restaurant...he's also been seen around town with her. Would you know anything about this?" Her grin was a bright as the sun.

He blushed, his whole face turning the darkest shade of red, and he looked away for a second with a smile that matched hers.

"I think I might know something about that." He murmured.

"You two make a cute couple, John, don't let her get away." Dottie whispered so that the others in the room couldn't hear her. "What do you need?"

John got down to business with the real reason why he was bothering her.

"I was wondering if you could give me the access code to trace the incoming calls on the regular, private office line for here. I need some information on a call that came in a while ago."

She reached for a Post It note and wrote the five-digit code in pen. As she handed it across the counter to him, she looked him in the eyes and smiled. "Remember, don't let her get away!"

The officer picked up the code, returned to the office computer, and typed in his access code and the numbers from the paper. The call log came up and he started working backwards, happy to realize that not many people used the regular line. Moving far enough back, he saw some calls that were not from private household or cellphone numbers. He started writing all the odd-looking numbers down. Going back six months he realized that he had about a dozen numbers that could not be easily identified.

Running another check on location, he found that a majority of the numbers were from the immediate area, but a couple were long distance from the Twin Cities. *"These are all probably numbers from cell phones, likely burners."*

John started calling the numbers on his list and found that almost all were answered or had answering services attached. Three numbers did not answer and they were from the immediate area. Taking note of the dates, the detective would make the assumption that a burner would be purchased locally at the Walmart on the edge of town.

"If the caller dialed the station on the same day that they bought the burner, I might be able to go out to Walmart and check their camera footage and maybe recognize the buyer of the phone. This could take a lot of time, but it could be very interesting!"

****

"I knew it, Travis...I just knew it! He killed Bruce! He's had his eyes on Faith for the longest time. We used to party with him every now and then and he was always hitting on her...you said you saw them together yourself. He had the device, he planted it, and he drove Bruce off the road...all so that he could be with Faith and collect the money. I knew it, I just knew it! Then he had to get rid of the device before I came looking for it. Faith tipped him off, so he put it back on the shelf...unbelievable! You solved it. Troy Haley killed Bruce!"

The young man listened carefully and said little. He wasn't sure what had really happened and Ed's explanation made sense. Still something seemed wrong and he couldn't seem to put his finger on what it was. He hung up after some more small talk and dozed off to sleep after surviving what felt like a very long day.

Chapter Twenty Nine

Rhonda Peterson was the prettiest girl in the Senior class and she wanted Travis Adamson really bad. Part of the reason had to do with the fact that he was among the best-looking boys in the school and had become Mr. Popular; the other reason was that Kim had his attention and heart. The challenge was too much for the Homecoming Queen to resist. She was going to chase him.

Travis and Danny both knew of her interest, but they also suspected that Travis would never leave his girlfriend. Dan and Susan were going steady and the two couples spent all their social time together. There was little chance that someone would break their group up, even if she was as stunning as Rhonda Peterson.

Winter Frolic week was a tradition at the school and, after a full week of activities, it culminated with the Frolic dance. Another ritual that had been handed down through the years was that the girls got to ask the boys to the dance and the boys could not turn an offer down. It was assumed that Kim would ask Travis, but on the first day of the week Rhonda Peterson was waiting at the end of the Adamson's driveway.

She stood directly in his path as he slowly backed out of the driveway and she wasn't going to budge. Travis looked in his rearview mirror and recognized her right away, but he had no idea what she was up to. It didn't take long for him to find out. He rolled down his window and said hello to the shivering young lady.

"Travis Adamson, will you accompany me to Frolic?" She was all smiles and he was temporarily taken with her beauty. Then his heart sank as he realized what had happened.

"But I am dating Kim...I can't go with you."

She frowned for a moment and then replied with a coy smile.

"Tradition states that the first person that asks you becomes your date...I think I'm first, right?"

He wanted to lie but something deep inside convinced him otherwise. *"Go with her! She's beautiful and it's only one night...Kim will understand!"* Travis had a strange feeling that Bruce was talking to him.

"I would be happy to go with you to Frolic."

Driving to school, Travis quickly realized that there would be hell to pay for this acceptance. He just didn't figure it would happen so quickly. He drove into the parking lot and pulled up next to Kim in her car.

"Trav, will you go with me to Frolic?" she asked in her flirtiest voice, already knowing what the answer would be.

"Uh, Kim...I gotta bit of a problem." Her expression fell as he explained what had happened in his driveway.

"I'm going to kill that bitch!" she screamed, loud enough for half the people in the lot to turn their heads toward her.

"Kimmy, settle down."

She glared at him. "Travis Adamson, don't you tell me to settle down!"

He reached out to her shoulder and gently pulled her close.

"So what? I have to go with her, big deal. I go with her and, after we arrive, you and I can spend the whole night dancing. There is no rule that says I have to dance with her all night. I only have to be her escort there. I'm sure she will run off with someone else once we start dancing the night away."

Kim looked up with him with skepticism in her eyes, but his smile melted her and she calmed down. They made their way arm in arm to the front entry. The morning flew by and before they knew it the lunch room was bustling with activity and they were sitting in the middle of it. Kim and Travis, Sue and Danny, just the way things were meant to be. Then the inevitable happened.

Rhonda Peterson crossed from one side of the room to the other, carrying her tray full of lunch. She purposefully moved up behind the foursome.

"Travis, I am really looking forward to our date on Saturday night."

Those were the words that sent Kim into a frenzy the likes of which Twin Lakes High School hadn't seen in years. Everything happened quickly.

"Rhonda Peterson, YOU ARE A BITCH!" Kim screamed as she spun and lunged with her lunch tray. The spaghetti flew off the tray and into Rhonda's face before she had time to react. Travis was frozen as well, he didn't turn until it was too late. Kim was now standing up, face to face with her antagonist and she swung the messy tray with full force into the side of Rhonda's head, dropping her to the floor.

The cafeteria was now on their feet and chants of "Fight! Fight!" were echoing off the brick walls. Everyone converged on the scene, blocking out the staff members who were supervising the room. Rhonda never got a swing in as Kim started kicking her with all her might. The girls were screaming and the Homecoming Queen was rolling under the tables trying to stay alive.

Mrs. Butwin, the physical education teacher dove into the pile and wrapped her arms around Kim. The profanity was flying from the young fighter and Rhonda was huddled under a table crying hysterically. Within the matter of a minute it was over and Travis' girlfriend was on her way to the Principal's office and a five-day suspension. There would be no Frolic dance for her this year.

Travis finished his lunch quickly and walked to fifth hour in a stupor. Danny and Sue were trying to console him, but he was having a hard time dealing with what he had just witnessed. Then the smile came over his face. He turned to Danny as they were about to part in the hallway.

"They were fighting over me!" Bruce was smiling and laughing inside of Travis' head and the world suddenly didn't seem so bad.

****

With his girlfriend suspended from school and the tradition of the dance, Travis knew he had to take Rhonda Peterson on Saturday night. His mom helped him pick out a suit and shoes for the special occasion and she even helped him tie his tie.

As darkness descended on the town, Travis made his way out to Lakeshore drive and pulled up in front of the Peterson house. Rhonda Peterson came from big money and the house reflected it; Travis' house could have fit inside it about five times.

He knocked on the front door and was met promptly by Rhonda's father. The older gentleman smiled and chuckled to himself, noting the nervousness on the younger man's face.

"You must be Travis! We have heard a lot about you, young man!" He held out his hand and Travis shook it with hesitation.

"I hope what you heard was good, sir." he replied in a meek tone. Mr. Peterson let out a deep laugh and nodded assuringly.

"If it hadn't been good, you wouldn't be taking my daughter to the dance!"

The father led the young suitor into the entry of the home and a look of pure astonishment covered Travis' face. The home was the most beautiful thing he had ever seen, the sheer grandiosity alone took him by surprise.

No sooner had he let his eyes survey the foyer than Rhonda appeared at the top of the stairs in front of him. She was absolutely the most beautiful girl he had ever seen. Travis' stunning date floated down the grand stairway with a smile and his gaze proved that he was mesmerized.

"Good evening, Travis. What do you think?" she purred, knowing that he was all caught up in her beauty.

"Wow, Rhonda...you look incredible." He turned toward the old man, hoping to not offend him with his comment about the daughter. Mr. Peterson just smiled.

"You kids had better get going right away, everything starts around seven." His tone turned much more severe as he laid out a reminder to the young man.

"Make sure you are home by midnight, not a minute later, you hear?" Travis nodded, understanding that the father meant all business with this suggestion.

Mrs. Peterson had come down the stairs behind her daughter but Travis was so focused on the young lady that he didn't notice her mom immediately. Her looks were reflected in Rhonda, she was also extremely attractive for her age and Travis caught himself staring at her a moment too long.

"We should get some quick pictures before you two go off to the dance…come over here and stand together."

Mrs. Peterson took plenty of pictures as the couple stood together and Travis couldn't take his eyes off Rhonda. She even smelled good and, when he put his arm around her, she melted right into him with a light laugh.

They were the perfect picture of the All-American Boy and the American Teenage Beauty Queen as they headed off to the school in Travis' car. His emotions seemed to be numb and then a sensation came over him as he looked at Rhonda, cuddled close to him in the front seat. *It was really good to be Travis Adamson at this moment.*" The young man could sense the old man in him beaming with pride.

When the couple entered the gymnasium for the big dance, everybody stared and admired them. Every high schooler at the dance wished they could be Travis and Rhonda…the people parted like the seas as they moved toward the center of the activity. The music started and

Rhonda moved against him, her eyes meeting his. They danced the rest of the night away.

The time flew by in the manner that it always does when one is having a great deal of fun. The young couple seemed to always be in the center of the social circle, the kids were massing around them and trying to be part of the 'in' crowd. While Travis liked this celebrity attention, he wished that he could be spending more time with Rhonda in private. The dance broke up at ten o'clock sharp and everyone planned to meet up at one of the many after dance parties across town.

With a half-dozen invitations to parties, the couple made their way to Travis' car and it soon became apparent that Rhonda had other plans.

"Let's go out by the point! There is always something fun happening there!" Travis turned his eyes toward her skeptically and answered in a more subdued manner.

"It's the middle of the winter, who in their right mind would be out there?"

She shrugged with a smile, working for a solid answer.

"I don't know, but there always seems to be something happening. C'mon, let's take a quick drive out there...we can hit a party in a bit. After all, we have until midnight, right?"

He couldn't resist her charm and he knew it was only a ten-minute detour. They made the drive in eight minutes and pulled into a deserted lot at a point that ran out into the lake. Travis parked the car and left the motor on, hoping that the heater would keep them warm.

Rhonda dialed in a soft music station on the radio and before he knew it she was all over him with kisses. There was no point in resisting and he knew he didn't want to stop, he had been hoping for something like this all night. If Travis had been himself he would have resisted out of fear and loyalty to Kim. Travis wasn't Travis, the older man had taken over.

The minutes flew by and he lost all track of the time. Peering at the dashboard from the backseat, he suddenly realized that it was eleven forty-five!

"Oh god! We are going to miss curfew...your dad is going to kill me!" Travis was back and was freaking out as he scrambled to assemble himself and move to the front seat. Rhonda was laughing and he couldn't figure out why.

"What's so funny? You're going to be in trouble too!" She sat up and straightened herself out, peaking into the mirror above the dash as she reached over the front seat.

"You have no idea where we are, do you?"

He mellowed slightly, taking note of her calmness.

"See those lights over there? Over across the cove? That's my house...I can walk there in five minutes...I think we will be ok. Chill out, will you? Come on back here, we can fool around for ten more minutes." Her eyes tempted him like he had never been tempted before.

"You're beautiful, you know that?" he countered as he moved into the driver's seat.

A squad car appeared at the entryway to the park and a spotlight was uncomfortably illuminating the inside of their car. The cop pulled up next to their car and moved around to the driver's window. Travis slowly rolled it down as it was hard to recognize who was standing there with the windows completely fogged up. The open window revealed Troy Haley in his work uniform. The smile that flashed across his face was priceless.

"You two behaving yourselves out here? It's a little cold to be parking at this time of the year, isn't it?" Rhonda was bothered by the dialogue and feeling guilty by getting caught, but Travis felt bold. The officer and him were on the same page, both exchanging knowing grins.

"Yes sir, it is a bit cold. I guess you could say we are behaving, within reason of course." Haley nodded and flashed his light toward Rhonda, obvious in his admiration, and she looked at him briefly and then looked away.

"You two be safe, you hear? It's a cold night to get stranded. Any problems just give us a call, ok?" The tone of the conversation took on a much more mellow tone and Travis knew everything was good.

"Yes, sir, officer Haley, any problems and we'll call." Troy Haley nodded reassuringly and walked back to his vehicle, eventually moving back onto the roadway.

"You are one cool dude, Travis Adamson, you know that?"

He just smiled with a confidence that could win any woman over. Travis realized that he had won her heart over during the course of the evening and now he had to scramble to get her back on time. They made it with five minutes left and the Frolic was a complete success.

Chapter Thirty

The Lakes County electrical truck sat idly in the circular driveway as the alarm suddenly rang. The intercom inside the big blue house filled the room with a mysterious voice.

"Identify yourself or disarm the alarm at the pad near the door!" it directed with a shrill that would freeze most home burglars. The intruder did not answer, instead he headed for the garage with his kit. The message was repeated two more times as the man settled in to work.

The alarm company out of Fargo put in a call to the police and Troy Haley was quickly on his way to Richwood to investigate. He recognized the address right away and knew that his girlfriend was in the cities; this was probably just another false alarm, the third in a week.

"Frickin' squirrels or some jacked up shit…damn alarms are useless." He muttered out of frustration as well as anger because he wished he was on his way to pay Faith a more enjoyable type of visit.

The officer stopped shorter than normal, near the bottom of the drive when he noticed the battered, old electrical truck.

"Geez, I thought they replaced these old things years ago. Must be a veteran electric man working on the screwed up system...probably been driving that thing since he started. Maybe Denny Frangham is working this one...he's older than Jesus."

Troy Haley had no concern whatsoever and figured he might have time to shoot the breeze with the old man...catch up on things that were happening over near the wildlife refuge where the weathered electrician lived with his old lady.

The front door was secure and the officer moved to the side of the residence and checked the service door to the garage; it was locked as well. Troy moved around to the back of the house, following footprints in the snow and reached the deck door with minimal effort. It opened right away, it was not locked.

"Hello? Anyone here? Twin Lakes Police, identify yourself!" There was no answer. "The old man is probably hard of hearing...he doesn't even know I'm here." Haley muttered aloud, hoping to not scare the guy into a heart attack.

Despite the house being chilly, the officer noted the cool breeze coming from the garage entry door on his left and he moved to shut it. Looking into the darkness of the car port, he flipped the light switch at the side of the door and the interior lit up. Troy Haley had no time to react, the flash caught him by surprise and he tumbled back into the kitchen in slow motion. One shot, a head shot, took his life almost instantly.

The assassin moved quickly to drag the officer's body into the kitchen; it would probably be an hour or more before the department figured out there was a problem with Haley. He pushed the garage door button and the opener whirred to life, lifting the panel door up to the ceiling. The squad was still running and he drove it into the garage to temporarily hide it.

Lowering the door, he had to hustle as he knew that the truck needed to be returned to the lot. It was one of the easiest things he had ever stolen, the keys were sitting in it and no one would probably miss it.

Re-setting the alarm took thirty seconds and within a minute the house was secured and he was making his way cautiously back through Richwood to Twin Lakes. He parked on a side street near the shopping mall and moved as normally as he could, he didn't want to arouse suspicion. He was an electrician calling it quits for the day and he would nonchalantly disappear into the night. No one had a clue.

****

Kim wasn't talking to Travis; for all she cared he could leave town and never come back. The word was out and everyone at Twin Lakes High School was talking about the dance and the hottest couple of the year. The boys were envious and the speculation over how far Travis had gotten with the town belle was reaching epic proportions.

It had been a week and a half since Frolic and it seemed that she had heard every story, every rumor. She had even seen the two of them together. She would cry at night by herself, but during the day she was as stoic as could be. If she ever had a chance to catch Rhonda Peterson alone though, a five-day suspension would not be adequate punishment.

Danny was staying away from the conflict and from Travis in general, he didn't fit the stereotype of the company that his friend was keeping and the fact that his girlfriend was best friends with Kim didn't help the situation.

Despite being the 'big man on campus' at Twin Lakes High, Travis suddenly felt very alone. His mind began to tell him that he was Rhonda Peterson's 'flavor of the month' and as soon as someone else came along he would be replaced. The strange feeling played itself out in another dream where Bruce was comparing Rhonda to his wife, Faith. Faith was the opposite of her name's definition, she was about as unfaithful as a woman could be.

He found the note on the table as he was settling down with an afternoon snack of Cap'n Crunch. He recognized his mother's handwriting but had yet to recognize her, a very strange conundrum for the young man. *"Call Dr. Emma right away. Something important has happened...don't wait or forget. Mom"* He grabbed his cell and punched up the number, wondering what was so urgent.

"Travis, I'm glad you called. Something crazy has happened out at Bruce's house. They found Troy Haley dead in the garage. Shot in the head... his car was inside the garage too. I wanted to tell you before you heard it somewhere else. John is meeting me at the diner, can you join us? He might have some things you might want to hear. Can you make it?" There was a pause as the young man took in all of the information, trying to process it as fast as he could.

"Why'd they kill Haley? That doesn't make sense. If he killed Bruce, who would want him dead? We're not even sure he killed Bruce? I'm confused." She waited for him to finish sorting things in his mind and then continued softly.

"I know all of this must be confusing to you, it's confusing me too. Just join us for dinner uptown...John might be able to shed some light on this for us. Will you join us?" Travis paused, he had nothing better to do as Rhonda was supposed to be doing something with her mom.

"Alright, what time?"

****

The trio was led to a booth in the back of the diner, where seclusion could work to their favor. No sooner had they settled down to order than Travis' phone beeped. He picked it up right away, noting the caller.

"Hi, Ed. What's up?" The man on the other line was more animated than normal.

"How are you doing kid? Everything going well for you? How's school?"

The older man's voice almost sounded too urgent for him, too eager.

"I guess things are pretty good up here. Went to the Frolic dance a couple of weeks ago with the hottest girl in the school." Travis was bragging the way Bruce would brag, plenty of manly bravado.

"Anything else new up there?"

Travis felt a strange sensation fall over him. *"Was there supposed to be something new to tell him. Should I mention Officer Haley?"* The pause on the line felt uncomfortable and he felt that Ed was impatient.

"YOU THERE TRAV?" He looked to Emma and John Buffalo sitting across from him and decided to lose Ed quickly.

"Look Ed, I have to go, I gotta run. Can I call you later? Maybe in a couple of hours?" There was a pause at the other end and Travis panicked. "Gotta go!"

He hung up the phone and wore a puzzled expression.

"That was Ed and he was really weird. He kept asking if there was anything new up here. So weird." Dr. Emma and Officer John exchanged knowing looks and then John spoke up.

"Travis, you're not going to believe this."

Chapter Thirty One

"I'm selling the god-damn place...my god Ed, they killed my boyfriend! I'm probably next! I wouldn't doubt if they are the same people that killed Bruce...it's probably those weird transplant people. I heard they take brains right out of the dead ones! I know they got Bruce's...I just know it! I'm next, Ed, I'm next!" She was hysterical on the phone, crying between declarations, wild with emotion.

"Just calm down, baby, everything will be alright...I will protect you." He tried to bring her down to a reasonable state with his assurances.

"How in the hell can you say that? Seriously, you could be dead too! We are all going to die, Ed!" He waited for a pause and the sobbing to start and then he interjected in his most compassionate voice possible.

"Look, baby, let me come over and see you. I will protect you. Let me drive over now."

Ed was trying his hardest to work his magic because with the right moves he could be with her tonight. He needed her bad, they hadn't been together in a long, long time.

"Look, honey, I'm on my way. Just stay there and don't do anything crazy. I will be there in a couple of minutes." He felt it deep in his mind, a conviction when she put down the phone.

"She's all mine now!"

****

The lights in the diner were fading as a reminder to the patrons that they would be closing in fifteen minutes. The waitress stopped by and asked if they needed anything before the kitchen shut down, another reminder to hurry them on their way. The trio had been sitting there for a long time and Travis couldn't seem to believe what he had heard. There was no way that John's theory was true. It was too hard for the young man to believe...too hard for Bruce to believe.

"Trav, what will it hurt to go through with the plan. If it works, we know who the killer is. If it doesn't, then there is really no harm done." The young man nodded at the cop and looked to his doctor as he gently pushed the empty soda glass away from him.

"What happens if I get attacked...if things go bad? Who will protect me?" He sounded like a little kid, not like the old man that was still in his head.

"Nothing is going to happen to you. I...I mean we...will be with you the whole way. Believe me, Trav, nothing is going to happen."

The next day seemed to drag on endlessly as Travis suffered through his classes. He tried to talk to Danny at lunch but they didn't seem to have much in common to talk about. The fact that Travis was dreading his four o'clock meeting at the police station also played on his mind and made him very quiet. As slowly as the day was moving, he wished it would move slower. The final bell rang and he left the chaos in the hallway quickly, hoping to grab a snack at home before the meeting.

No one was home when he entered the back door. "Sylvia? Sylvia? Are you home?"

There was no answer, just the hum of the appliances in the house. He missed the woman that was supposedly his mom even though he still couldn't remember anything about her. This made him even more frustrated and the headaches were getting harder to bear. Somedays he wished that he could just crawl in a hole and die; he felt so alone.

As he opened the old refrigerator he suddenly realized that his appetite was lacking and so he shut the door with a little too much force. He could hear bottles clanging and something fall to the bottom but he was too disinterested to check. Leaving his overfilled backpack on the kitchen table, he pivoted back out the door, making sure to check that it was locked.

A quick call to Sylvia seemed to settle his mind; she reminded him of why she was working so many extra hours and that college could be very expensive. He was grateful for her care and dedication and he let her know how

255

important her sacrifices were to him. By the time he parked at the police station he was in a better mood.

He pulled up a chair in a general use office at the end of the bright tiled corridor and both Officer Buffalo and Doctor Emma were already there to greet him.

"I made the call to Faith earlier today, informing her that her lake residence was the site of a crime and she assured me that she would be here in the morning. I used a bunch of legalese and made sure to let her know that she is not considered a suspect. She was very agitated, nervous, but she said she would be here by ten."

Emma cut in, hoping to keep Travis calm.

"You won't have to deal with Faith at all. She will be kept here and questioned by another officer...general routine stuff regarding our access to her property. It will be during this time that she will give us free access to the property and so we will need no warrant. Smooth as silk." She smiled reassuringly and the young man settled back in a more comfortable posture.

"Your job will be to get Ed out to the lake home. Tell him you need to see him. He will travel up with Faith and all we have to do is get them apart. Whatever it takes, get him out to the lake home." Travis frowned; he was not sure he could convince the old man to come up much less meet him at the blue house.

"I don't know. This sounds really difficult." The two adults in the room looked at each other and then back at the kid. Emma took her turn trying to bolster his confidence.

"Just tell him you want to see him, to talk about old times, whatever. I know you can do it. Remember, you are his best friend Bruce...he will welcome the opportunity to see you instead of the police."

Travis slipped back into his Bruce persona as he dialed his best friend's number by heart.

"Ed, I didn't get a chance to get back to you the other night. Sorry old man. Is everything alright?" The young kid was channeling Bruce and his voice even sounded a little older. The cop and doctor exchanged impressed glances and then focused back on the kid.

"Yeah, yeah. I know. I heard all about it." He was in dialogue with Ed and was hearing him out.

"Hey, you have to come up tomorrow. I don't want to go out to the house alone...it's a crime scene. It's supposedly somewhat cleaned up, but I am really kind of freaked out about the whole thing."

There was a pause as Ed was rambling on about the shame of it all.

"I know, yeah, I know. Come on up." Pause. "Great, come up with Faith then. It will be good to see her."

Another pause and chatter on the other end of the line that the doctor and officer could not make out.

"Police station, huh? Probably standard stuff. Drop her off with the cops and meet me out at the house." More chatter in a gentler tone. "Ten thirty would be great...I'm really looking forward to seeing you, buddy."

They wrapped up the conversation and Travis signed off. He was met by gentle clapping from his colleagues as they were beyond impressed with his role.

"It is done then. Ten tomorrow morning here and ten thirty at the house with you and Ed. Let's run out and get the lay of the place." Travis smiled, hoping deep down that Ed was innocent but unsure just the same.

"I know the place like the back of my hand. Hell, I built most of it with my own two hands." Smiles permeated the room as they noisily slid their wooden chairs back from the table and made for the door. Tomorrow would be an interesting day.

Chapter Thirty Two

Travis returned to the comfort of a home-cooked dinner and the reality of what tomorrow could bring slowly unsettled his mind. By the end of the meal he was feeling restless; Trav knew he had to talk to Danny and set their friendship on the right path again. He dialed the number and waited for an answer, not sure of what he was going to say. His friend picked up with a standard "hello?".

"Hey Dan."

"Hey Trav, what's up?"

"I was wondering if you wanted to go fishing tonight, out at the blue house...nobody's home." There was a hesitation on the other end.

"Geez, Trav, I don't know. It seems like every time we go near the place something crazy happens. Why do you want to go there? I heard a cop was killed out there." A pause ensued and Travis struggled for words.

"Yeah, that's right. The cop that almost killed us in his garage was shot out there. It's all over now...there is nobody there and we don't have to go inside. I just thought it would be fun to hang out like old times and throw a line in the water."

His friend didn't know what to think about the invitation; they had not been spending much time together since Travis broke up with Kim.

"C'mon, it'll be fun." Another pause.

"I guess it would be a good time. When are you thinking of going?"

Fifteen minutes later Travis pulled up in his beater and the boys headed for Richwood and the blue house by the lake. A quick stop at the general store produced a plastic bag of minnows and within a half hour they were in a small, aluminum boat with an old outboard motor hanging off the back.

They pulled into the bay at the corner of the long, angular lake and they dropped a rusty anchor over the side. Both boys set up their fishing rigs and began watching their baited lines in eight feet of water. Silence overtook them for a few minutes and then Travis began to speak from his heart.

"You're my best friend, you know that?"

Dan looked up from the lake and smiled at his pal across the boat. Travis continued.

"I'm really sorry that I have been treating you so lousy…I guess I really got tangled up with Rhonda and forgot about what was important. I should have been a better friend."

The stillness of the lake was only overshadowed by the light breeze moving through the trees. An occasional gust of wind would stir the boat as it passed over the cold, spring time water and it inflicted a chill on the fishermen.

Dan shivered for a moment, wishing that he had brought a better jacket, and then shrugged toward his friend.

"Don't worry about it, Trav. If Rhonda Peterson was chasing me I probably would have done the same thing. So what's the deal with you two?"

Travis noted the change in the topic and suddenly realized that things were good with his best friend.

"She dumped me for Tommy Crawford, the new kid that transferred from Fargo. I always kinda knew she would drop me sooner or later, but it was fun while it lasted."

The friends exchanged smiles and a knowing chuckle between them.

"It looks like things are good with you and Sue, huh?"

Dan couldn't hide a wider smile and he began to blush.

"It's good…she's good…I mean we're good." He wanted to change the topic again as he was uncomfortable talking about his love life.

"Kim still misses you. Will you ever try to get back together with her? She was in love with you."

The possibilities of reunion were discussed and now it was Travis who was trying to change the topic.

"Hey, pull up your line and watch this. You have to see this to believe it."

They reeled in their fishing gear and Travis took the small, black device out of his tackle box. He set a controller on the seat next to him and hooked the box to the motor, steering mechanism, and battery in the back of the boat.

A quick pull of the starting rope set the motor purring and he flipped a switch on the controller. Dan pulled up the anchor and they began moving from the bay onto the main lake. Travis took his hand off the steering mechanism and began maneuvering the hand-held controller. He was steering the boat by remote and Dan was enthralled.

"What in the world is that?" Travis was proud of Bruce's invention.

"This, my friend, is the original prototype for the RAD and RAD2. I first tested it on this very boat about ten years ago…I'm surprised it still works!"

The boys took turns playing with the device and finally made it back to shore. They stowed the controller and their fishing gear in the small boathouse near the dock and made their way back to town as the sun was setting in the western sky. It was good to be best friends again.

Chapter Thirty Three

She was nervous as she entered the front doors of the Twin Lakes police station, but one would never know it. Faith carried herself with an air of confidence and every officer in the place was checking her out. They couldn't help themselves, she exuded sex.

Ed closed the sedan door behind her and looked her over as well. His smile told the whole story. He had consoled her at her place the evening before and he got everything he wanted and more.

"It's SO good to be Fast Eddie!"

He headed north out of town, keeping his eyes on the road and on his speedometer. It was easy to speed on Richwood Road and he didn't need any cops hassling him on this sunny morning. He checked his shoulder holster and his pistol, nodding calmly with the note to his mind that the problem would be over in a matter of an hour or two.

"Brucie old boy, I killed you once and I guess I will have to do it again."

He pulled onto the circular, concrete driveway and parked next to the kid's vehicle. He made a mental note to get rid of the junker later; now it was time to get rid of the kid. He shut his door quietly and approached the front of the big, blue home. Travis opened the door and met him with a friendly greeting and a handshake on the expansive white porch.

"Come on in, Ed. It's so good to see you!"

The men left the open porch for the privacy and comfort of the house. Ed settled down on the couch as Travis poured him a drink and grabbed a Coke for himself. It didn't take long for the stories of times gone by to change to the present situation. The young man took a sip, paused to study the older man, and then hit him with the million-dollar question.

"Ed, why did you kill me?" The older man sat in stunned silence for a moment, calculating his situation and answer.

"What do you mean, Travis? I would never kill you...you're right here, alive?" Travis feigned a smile and felt a slight disgust at his supposed friend.

"Cut the shit, Ed. This is Bruce talking. I know you killed me, it doesn't take a fucking brain surgeon to figure it out."

The boy waited for a reaction and saw the reality hit the old man's face. Then he continued on his line of reasoning out loud.

"Look, I know you had a thing for Faith…it was so damned obvious. You drool down the front of your shirt every time you see her…I don't blame you, mind you, but come on… she's my wife. Second, you knew how to operate the RAD2 as well as I did…no one else could run it well enough to crash the car. You had access to my car in order to plant the damn thing and you knew I would never suspect it."

Travis was in full Bruce mode now, ticking off the facts with his fingers in an animated manner to tick Ed off.

Ed was listening to his old friend, but deep inside his mind was reeling as he was ready to shoot him between the eyes. Travis continued as Bruce, setting him off further.

"Third, you took the RAD2 before the cops showed up…only you could remove it that fast, even if you left part of it under the dash in the fuse box. By the time Troy Haley showed up you were already gone. He had figured it out though, didn't he? Somehow, or at least you thought he did because you killed him right here. His ghost is probably watching you right now. Creepy huh?"

The old man lowered his eyes for a moment, the guilt evident in his posture. He looked up slowly and stared down Travis with intense hatred. Travis, aka Bruce, wasn't finished yet and he was becoming more animated with each accusation.

"What the hell, Ed…did you have to KILL ME? I would have given you Faith, she's nothing but a slut anyhow...totally unfaithful! But NO, there was more. You could sell the RAD2 and take your half of the profit, but you had to have it all. You had to have MY half as well...you had to have it ALL!"

Something inside of Travis' mind snapped and he began to tear up, to break down in front of his friend as he realized that he was right. His best friend in the whole world had killed him. His eyes focused on the floor and his shoulders began to heave as he sobbed quietly, caught in the reality of his fate.

Ed moved his hand to his shoulder holster and paused to let his victim compose himself. He would be killing a kid, but he would also be re-killing the old friend who had figured him out.

"You know, Bruce, there really is no reason to deny what you said." The weapon appeared from his jacket and now was leveled at the young man across the coffee table.

"You're right. I can't believe you put this all together, but you did. I should have known that you would figure it out sooner or later. I thought the cop did, but he probably didn't have a clue. It felt good to kill him because he was stealing Faith away from me. One shot...boom, all over. I guess that will be the same for you."

Travis felt his stomach rise to his throat and he moved his lips to speak but no words were coming out. He began to wonder what he had gotten himself into as a feeling of intense dread came over him. Ed sank back in the sofa a bit and continued his tirade.

"You just don't get it, do you? You had everything...the trophy wife, the wealth, the athletic stardom, the brains, everything. You always had everything and you didn't cherish it, you didn't deserve it...you took it for GRANTED. I had to sit there, every single day, and watch you live the life that I worked for, that I DESERVED. I never had what you did, but I could have Faith and she's a pretty good start. I could have the wealth, all of it. Your time was up, your luck ran out." He stopped and looked with a small bit of pity at the kid seated across from him.

"You know kid, I really wish you hadn't figured all of this out. I like you...you are kind of like a son to me." He played with the gun in his hand, waving it nonchalantly. "We have a lot in common...both of us have had to fight to get what we have. Your only problem is that half of your brain is Bruce and now I need to finish him again. It's nothing personal, kid...I just have to do it."

The weapon began to rise toward Travis and he felt faint, the room was spinning and getting dark.

"Freeze Ed! Don't move or I'll blow your head off!"

John Buffalo emerged from the small office off to the side of the living room with a shotgun leveled at Ed's head. Time stood still as everyone froze and Travis slumped over on the couch. The officer turned slightly in surprise, confused as to why the young man fell on his side and Ed fired a shot at him. The bullet struck John Buffalo in the shoulder and his shotgun fired into the ceiling as he fell backward.

The commotion brought Travis back to life, but there was nothing he could do. Ed was headed across the kitchen and out the back door to the lake, confused about what to do next. The old man ran for the shoreline and jumped into the fishing boat at the side of the dock.

John Buffalo got back onto his feet and realized that he was lucky, the bullet hit mostly vest and grazed his arm. Regaining his senses, he began the pursuit with Travis at his side.

Ed pulled the rope and the motor sprang to life. He realized that he had to get away quickly; he was no match for the lawman. His mind reeled in confusion as he had no idea what to do next.

The boat began moving away from the shore toward the middle of the lake. John Buffalo dropped his shotgun and pulled his pistol from his holster. The shot seemed too far but he tried anyway and missed his target.

Ed heard the shot and panicked, the officer was still alive and pursuing him. He looked back to see both the men disappearing into the boathouse. *"What in the hell are they doing?"*

The pair emerged and moved onto the dock. Suddenly the motor slowed down and began to spin the boat in circles.

"This thing has gone haywire! I can't control it! Shit!"

The outboard motor suddenly roared to full speed and Ed fought with the steering handle to no avail. He looked to shore and saw Travis holding a remote control and grinning; the pair was now moving quickly to take cover behind the boat shack.

The small vessel was careening out of control, rolling with and then against the waves, bouncing along at too fast a speed. Ed let out a yell that was drowned out by the screaming motor. He was headed straight for the dock and now took both hands off the steering wheel, covering his head in an attempt to protect and brace himself for impact.

Travis and John heard the panicked scream, a last-ditch cry for help. The small aluminum boat was no match for the heavy wooden dock and it hit head on, flipping end over end. Ed's body was hurled through the air and he landed directly on his head at the shoreline end of the wooden structure. His neck twisted and cracked and his cranium began to bleed profusely. He didn't move, he just laid flat on the front of his body and twitched.

"I think I killed him!" Travis muttered in an out of body experience of sorts.

"Yeah, you might have killed him." John retorted, holding his sore shoulder, gun draped at his side. "Run up to the house and call for an ambulance. I will see what I can do."

Travis dropped the controller and sprinted up the lawn to the big structure, freaked out over what he had just done. Halfway to the blue house he began to laugh hysterically. Travis' sprint became a walk; he was in no hurry to save the man who had killed him.

He returned to the shore to find Ed laying on his back, totally immobile while John did his best to stop the bleeding from his forehead. The old man was breathing and his eyes were looking all around, but nothing else was moving. His lips began to move and he started to whisper. His voice slowly got louder as he focused on the young man holding a phone. Ed began blubbering.

"I'm sorry Bruce, so sorry Bruce."

John looked to the young man standing over him, whose color was returning to his face. Trav's appearance was eerie and the officer felt as if he saw someone else suddenly standing in front of him.

"Do you want to say anything to him before the ambulance gets here and takes him to town?" Travis looked at Ed for a long moment and then replied in a cold, dead manner.

"Payback is a bitch. Get him the fuck out of here."

The voice was one hundred percent Bruce.

Chapter Thirty Four

Both lawyers sat across the table from the trio, the older lawyer appeared unkempt but savvy while the younger one was dressed like a model from GQ but was as quiet as a church mouse. Travis felt special to be included in this hearing even though it was brought on by the threat of a lawsuit from Ed Payne. Doctor Emma and John Buffalo were sitting on each side of him, keeping him happy and calm.

The senior lawyer started the conference with a simple question, delivered in a nonchalant manner.

"I am assuming that your friends have informed you about the nature of this meeting?" He turned his attention to the doctor and policeman and they nodded in the affirmative.

"You are being sued by Mr. Edward Payne concerning an event that caused him bodily harm...permanent paralysis to be exact, for the sum of ten point five million dollars. This doesn't include medical expenses or rehabilitation. He is also claiming patent infringement...theft of his device patent to the tune of twenty million dollars plus all revenue from the said device. Total sum in the case should be in the neighborhood of fifty million dollars."

Travis was stunned by the monetary figure and traded quick glances with his friends.

"This is a joke, right? Right?" He paused and realized the seriousness of the situation.

"He stole the product from me after killing me and then he tried to steal every aspect of my life. There is no way he is going to win fifty mil." The lawyers both nodded in agreement and continued on their path of discussion.

"You need not worry. We have all the evidence we need to debase his claim and prove that he was a fugitive fleeing the police during the accident...it was an accident, right?" The senior lawyer flashed an evil smile as he quietly murmured the last part of his comment. Travis nodded with a smile and the process continued further.

"We feel we have more than enough evidence to charge Mr. Payne with at least three murders, attempted murder, insurance fraud, and possible patent theft. What does the docier list, Mr. Caldwell?" The young lawyer now spoke up and was obviously very meticulous and smart.

"It seems that, according the records here, you two got Mr. Payne to give verbal incrimination of himself...on record I might add. The recording device planted in the room was a splendid idea. The wound that Officer Buffalo received works in your favor, as well as some other facts that the fine officer recovered. Would you care to explain further, Officer Buffalo?"

The big man now took his turn relaying the facts of his investigation into the matter.

"I checked all the phone calls that would have come in to Officer Haley and then began going through records looking for burner phones. After finding possible burner numbers, I then checked phone sales in town and found a few from the local Walmart. By checking video surveillance I was able to identify with certainty Mr. Payne. I wasn't sure if he bought one of the phones, but it sure looked like it…at least I know he was in the store prior to the call."

Everyone at the table nodded with encouragement as he paused to take a drink of water and compose his words.

"Another piece of the puzzle comes from something you told me." He looked over at Travis as he pointed in his direction. "You said that you found the RAD2 on the shelf in the garage at the lake home. You had been in there before and had not seen it, right?"

Travis nodded again, thinking back to his break in with Danny and the girls.

"Yet, after Ed called you and asked to check again it mysteriously shows up in a place where you would have surely seen it the time before. Ed wanted you to find the RAD2…he planted it with hopes of framing Todd Haley. He also called Seth Emery and shot him twice, killing him and then burying the body just east of the lake home in a swamp…I guess you guys already know that. We think that

Seth knew what the device was and had begun to unravel the mystery."

"How would Seth know about any of this?" Emma asked, hoping that her colleague wasn't involved in the mess.

"It is believed that Seth knew Bruce and Ed. He had seen the RAD2 demonstrated...we asked Faith, Bruce's wife about this and she remembered him hanging out and playing with the device during a summer party or two. She also admitted to pursuing him with romantic intent...she was quite attracted to the young man."

The senior attorney nodded with encouragement to his junior assistant, they traded smiles, and Caldwell continued.

"Seth wanted a piece of the action. He knew that Ed was the chief suspect and he called Ed to extort money from him, or at least to become part of the deal for the RAD2. We can't confirm this, but it makes sense. Ed met him and killed him to get him out of the way."

Bruce was screaming deep in Travis' mind, he couldn't believe that his wife would cheat on him with a young man that they had only recently met. Then he realized that his wife had invited Seth to many of their get-togethers. She was trying to cheat on him all the way back then and he was too caught up in himself and his interests to even notice. Travis grabbed at his temples with both hands and began to feel nauseous.

"I need a break…I need some water." He got up from the table quickly and moved to the corridor in search of a water fountain. Emma followed and tried to help him cope with all the information he had just had forced upon him. She caught up with him at the fountain and saw the tears at the edge of his eyes.

"Doc, she was cheating on him with Seth and Troy…she was cheating on me during our whole marriage. Love sucks, Doc…love just sucks!" He broke down in tears and she held him in a comforting embrace.

"Just let it go, Trav…let it go."

Chapter Thirty Five

"Dan, she was cheating on me with Seth and Troy, both of them...she's just like Rhonda."

His best friend was sitting on the edge of the brick wall at the end of the boardwalk, looking out at the expansive Twin Lake. A couple of late 60's muscle cars roared by on the lake drive on their way to the center of the town and they took a moment to admire the beautiful machines before Travis continued.

"Ed killed Seth and then set up a burglary at the lake house to kill Todd. He killed both because of the affairs and the money from the RAD2 deal. Unbelievable."

Dan interrupted suddenly as he was caught up in the story. "How do they know he killed Troy Haley?"

Travis turned to him and smirked, already ahead of his friend. With a knowing glance, he moved on.

"A woman who was walking her golden retriever saw a Wild Rice Electric truck parked in the driveway of the blue house. It was stolen and the lot at Wild Rice has cameras. Ed was identified easily by video."

"Why didn't they bust him right away then?" Travis provided more of the story with confidence.

"She didn't think anything of it or come forward until well after the fact. John Buffalo walked the whole area and found her after our shootout."

The boys fell silent for a bit and returned their attention to the cars on the street and the pretty girls crossing the thoroughfare to the beach.

"Ed had the RAD2 the whole time but he knew that if he came forward to make the deal with Illinois for twenty million he would be busted with the evidence from Bruce's murder. He had to make it look like Troy had it and put it back on the shelf, then I could find it and return it to him. He would get rid of Troy and then he could take the repaired device to Chicago and seal the deal. It was all about love and money. I don't want to grow up, life is too weird. Growing up sucks."

Then Travis let out a low laugh, one that invoked images of Bruce. Dan had seen this transformation before and he knew instantly that Bruce was back.

"It was so crazy though…he hit the dock and flipped way the hell up into the air. Huge air! When he landed all you could hear was the crack and thud of him…broken neck and all. I had all I could do to keep from laughing! It was so wicked!"

Danny looked sideways at his best friend and, for a moment, was very scared of him.

****

He saw her across the crowded cafeteria and he wanted to get back together with her so badly it hurt. She was on his mind all the time and he found himself following her in the hallways between classes. He even walked by her house at night, hoping to catch a glimpse of her, to hear her voice like music on the night air.

Spring was turning to summer and school would be out in a week with a graduation ceremony finalizing his time at Twin Lakes High School. He wanted to finish it with her.

He moved up behind her in the lunch line and spoke softly.

"Hey beautiful, can I join you for lunch?"

She knew he was behind her and she wasn't going to fall for his charms too easily.

"It's a free world, there's nothing stopping you."

It was a cold comment, but there was a slight air of encouragement contained within it. They moved to their old table and joined Danny and Sue; the surprise on the faces of everyone at the table could not be hidden.

Awkward silence gave way to the small talk and gossip that permeates most high school lunch tables and when the half hour break was up Travis decided to make his move. He gently moved her aside in the crowded hallway and looked her in the eyes.

"Kim, I really want to see you. I am so sorry about everything. Can we just go somewhere and talk?"

She looked at him, looked away for a moment, and then spoke with determination, almost like an order.

"Follow me. We're going to cut fifth hour. Move."

A smile crossed both their faces as they bolted out the side door and into the bright sunshine. It was much more fun to be high school kids.

The class cutters made sure to steer clear of the gym class that was going out toward the open field on the south side of the school. They wound through the parking lot and ended up at the top of the football bleachers, leaning against the press box that shielded them from the view of the high school. The couple sat quietly, eyes closed for a minute or two, just soaking in the warmth of the sun. Then she spoke.

"I heard you are going to be a new dad. Sounds like Rhonda has a bun in the oven. Travis Adamson is going to have a little Travis to take care of."

His heart fell with her comment. She smiled, knowing that she was toying with him.

"The kid is not mine, swear to God, it's Tommy Crawford's kid. They have been together since right after Frolic...I swear it's not my kid!"

She laughed that evil laugh that always made Travis laugh too, she knew he was telling the truth and he realized he had been played.

"Shut up or you will get us busted!" she whispered with emphasis. "The last thing I need is more detention."

Chapter Thirty Six

The graduation ceremony arrived on a pleasantly cool Friday night during the first week of June. The graduates were assembled outside of the gymnasium dressed in their formal gowns and caps and excitement filled the air.

The music began and they filed into the crowded venue side by side while the traditional tune, "Pomp and Circumstance", echoed throughout the building. The high school band had been practicing this piece over and over for the last three months and it sounded pretty good.

Travis found his memory flashing back many years to a day where he walked into a great church on a college campus and completed his storybook college career. His best friend was with him and some of their closest buddies were all assembled on the great lawn in front of the building for pictures. Life couldn't get any better than at that moment; nothing but new possibilities and plenty of fun. His mind would suddenly snap back into the present and the headache would get a little stronger. If he closed his eyes for a minute or two it would all go away.

He looked over at the friends in the other line as he walked and he spotted Rhonda a few people ahead. The gown hid her bump, but everyone in the place knew that she was walking with an additional person. Tommy Crawford was almost directly next to him and for a brief second Travis almost felt sorry for him.

The pity faded almost instantly as he realized that Tommy Crawford got what he deserved. As the graduates in front of him sat down row by row in the middle of the gym, he continued toward the front where the kids with the last names starting with A, B, and C would be.

He smiled as he passed Kim and she smiled back. Everything was good. He nodded at Danny and the gesture was returned. Again, everything was good. He arrived at his spot and took a seat on the padded chair while the music stopped. The headache suddenly hit him like a hammer on the back of his head and he almost fell forward off his chair. The classmate next to him grabbed him and steadied him on his seat.

"You alright, Travis?"

Trav kept his eyes closed and nodded his head slowly.

"Yeah, I'm fine, just a case of the nerves and heat in here." He laughed half-heartedly to convince his classmate that he was fine.

The pain was not going away, it was becoming more intense. Travis had trouble focusing on the stage and his mind kept wandering back to a beautiful auditorium that felt very familiar. He saw classmates he recognized, but they looked different.

Bruce's name was announced and he moved across a small stage and shook hands with Mr. Wentworth, the principal. In his left hand was placed a small but impressive looking diploma. Hibbing High School was written in gold across the front of the document and his name, Bruce D. Nickel, was scrolled in fine black script in the center. Cameras flashed as he smiled and waved to the large crowd that clapped just a little bit louder for him.

His brain returned to the crowded gymnasium and the kid sitting next to him nudged him more aggressively the second time.

"C'mon Travis, it's our turn!" he repeated urgently as the spectators all stared.

"Oh, sorry Sam." the daydreamer replied with embarrassment.

He shuffled quickly toward the stage and caught up with the rest of the group. His eyes wandered in this new setting and he spotted Sylvia, Emma, and Big John a few rows up to his left in the bleachers. He nodded and smiled as he approached the steps to the stage.

Ascending one careful step at a time, he moved toward the principal and superintendent as his name was called out. Admirers in the senior class let out a few yelps and he shook hands with the officials and received his diploma.

Travis paused to survey his classmates waiting their turn in seats behind his row, waved his document, and blew a kiss toward Miss Weston. The graduates erupted in cheers and he received a blushing smile from the young teacher seated in the faculty section. This time it was all Travis...no Bruce.

The ceremony was over much more quickly than any of the young honorees expected. One minute they were the senior class of Twin Lakes and now they were the newest alumni, ready to go out and conquer the world. Hats flew, hugs were exchanged, and the school rouser played loudly as the group scurried out of the gym to loud cheers. Travis made his way to Kim, Dan, and Susan as fast as he could. This was a moment he wanted to cherish; he knew it would never come again.

Chapter Thirty Seven

Travis' ears were ringing, he needed a glass of cold water and a dark room. He moved quietly through the house, not wanting to wake or alarm his mother on a slow Saturday morning. With his index fingers pressing on his temples, he moaned in a hushed manner and finally found his way into the bathroom. The light was intense and the white, porcelain bathroom fixtures gave off a gleam that hurt his eyes.

He stood in front of the pedestal sink and squinted into the mirror. Travis sensed something was wrong and he feared for the worst; he grasped the sides of the sink and looked intensely at himself for a minute, trying to focus on the situation and ignore the pounding in his skull. An image stared back at him and he recoiled slowly to focus; an older man with gray hair and facial stubble was smiling at him and nodding.

It was Bruce Nickel. The image was saying something to him but he couldn't hear it; he would know Bruce's voice as it had reverberated through his mind so many times before. Whatever was being said seemed to be reassuring, but the young man just stared at his old image. Bruce nodded to him with a smile and Travis found himself smiling back.

"Goodbye."

The old man nodded with one last motion and was gone.

The room spun wildly out of control and Travis saw the pattern on the ceiling rotate and fall away. He grabbed for the edge of the sink and felt the cold porcelain slide across the palms of his hands. He corkscrewed gently to the floor and everything went black.

****

They stood around the bed in an eerie stillness, as quiet as they could be. Gentle sobs were the only noises one could perceive, aside from an occasional announcement from the hall way. One by one, each visitor made their way out with Danny consoling Kim who was sobbing much louder as she retreated. Emma Harris had stopped earlier and was now making a quick check of her patients before she could return.

The coma had taken Travis from them over a month ago and now the only thing left to do was wait for the inevitable. With vital signs deteriorating suddenly, a transfer to a hospice was out of the question. Dr. Harris had never encountered this situation before and she suspected that the complications her patient was enduring stemmed from the football concussion as much as the transplant.

His mother, Sylvia Adamson, was the last remaining person in the room. The patient shifted slightly and she did a double take, not sure she had just seen what had happened. Travis was breathing erratically, his chest heaving, and his mouth moved to say something but no noise came out.

She reached out and held his hand as his chest stopped moving. There was suddenly no breath, no movement. Sylvia waited and said a silent prayer as the awareness of finality hit her. She looked at her son's face and whispered "Travis." Her eyes fell to his hand in hers and tears started streaming down her cheeks.

The young man's hand tensed and his eyes slowly opened to see his mother falling apart emotionally. "Mom, what's wrong?"

The End

Acknowledgements

As with most literary works of this nature, there are many people to thank…too many to actually list! I would like to give special thanks to Roberta Arvidson and Samantha Andresen for their editing skills and great advice. I could always count on Bertie and Sam to give me honest, quality input in regard to my work. Special thanks are also due to my family for putting up with my solitude while writing, many times when I was probably needed around the house!

I have been blessed with a wonderful wife who understands my need to create and has continued to put up with my crazy ideas and unpredictable mood swings, not to mention having to put up with my constantly changing stories and ideas. Sarah, you're the best!

Thank you to the people who have continued to support my dream by buying my books, you always make my day and enable me continue my craft. A book in not worth much if nobody reads it; my followers make my books invaluable.

A final thanks to my publisher, Northern Star, for putting these projects together. These books would never see the light of day without them and KDP, the printer and peddler of my work.

On a separate note, if any agents are interested in backing a published writer with a million more ideas coming to fruition, give me a call and maybe we can work together and build this dream further!

About The Author

D.J. Hamlin is a published writer through Northern Star Publishing and "Transplant" is his third novel. Specializing in historical fiction, this work is the first of Hamlin's to feature a futuristic mystery storyline. In addition to "Transplant", the author has also written a thrilling spy series that includes "The Middle Man" and "Half A World Away", both of which feature the fictional character Brian Konrad. When he is not writing, D.J. teaches Social Studies and coaches football in the beautiful state of Minnesota.

Other Works by D.J. Hamlin

The Middle Man, The Brian Konrad Series, Book One, 2019

Half A World Away, The Brian Konrad Series, Book Two, 2019

Also Coming Soon: **The Visitor**, The Brian Konrad Series, Book 3, Anticipated release in the Summer of 2020.

"Stand Up and Cheer: 75 Years of Packer Hockey" A history of the famed high school hockey program in South St. Paul, Minnesota. Anticipated release in the Fall of 2020.